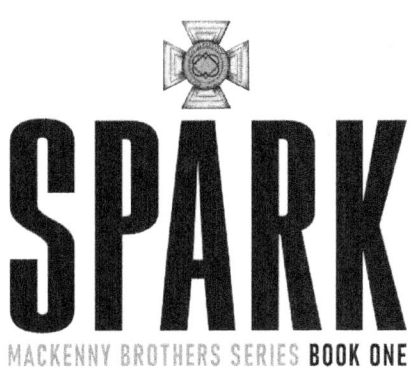

SPARK
MACKENNY BROTHERS SERIES **BOOK ONE**

KATHLEEN KELLY

Spark
MacKenny Brothers Book 1

Kathleen Kelly

This book is a work of fiction. Any references to real events, real people, and real places are used fictitiously. Other names, characters, places and incidents are products of the Author's imagination and any resemblance to persons, living or dead, actual events, organisations or places is entirely coincidental.

All rights are reserved. This book is intended for the purchaser of this book ONLY. No part of this book may be reproduced or transmitted in any form or by any means, graphic, electronic, or mechanical, including photocopying, recording, taping, or by any information storage retrieval system, without the express written permission of the Author. All songs, song titles and lyrics contained in this book are the property of the respective songwriters and copyright holders.

All efforts have been made to ensure the correct grammar and punctuation in the book. If you do find any errors, please e-mail Kathleen Kelly: kathleenkellyauthor@gmail.com
Thank you.

Disclaimer: The material in this book contains graphic language and sexual content and is intended for mature audiences, ages 18 and older.

ISBN: 978-1707154494

Editing and Proofreading by Swish Design & Editing
Book design by Swish Design & Editing
Cover design by Clarise Tan at CT Cover Creations
Cover image Copyright 2019
First Edition 2018
Second Edition 2019
Copyright © 2019 Kathleen Kelly
All rights reserved.

DEDICATION

To my long-suffering husband. You are my everything. Without your constant support and love, I would still be wandering around this planet wondering what the hell I'm doing here.

You make the darkest days lighter.

Infinity plus one.

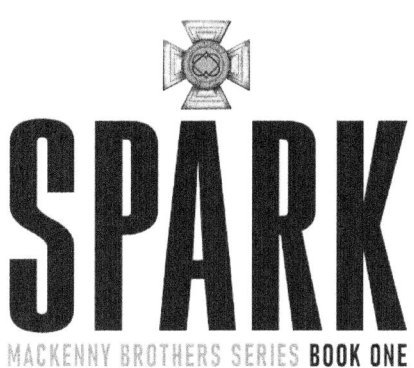

SPARK

MACKENNY BROTHERS SERIES **BOOK ONE**

PROLOGUE

"Maddock! Maddock, open the door."

It's barely seven o'clock in the morning, and my kid sister, Heather, is pounding on my front door. I have a piece of toast in my mouth and a coffee in my hand as I fling the door open. I take a bite of the toast and wave it at her. "Jesus, Heather, what do you want?"

Pushing past me, she goes into the kitchen and picks up my other piece of toast. "Is that any way to talk to your favorite sister?"

"You're my *only* sister, and that's my breakfast."

Heather smirks at me and takes a bite. I shake my head at her and take a sip of my coffee.

"Why are you here? Apart from eating my food?"

"Toast for breakfast is bad for you, anyway. It's all carbs. You don't want to get fat, do you?"

"Heather?"

"My car is making a stupid noise again. Could you look at it?"

"Love, I have a big meeting this morning at work. I *can't* be late."

"Fine, drop me to work then."

I shake my head. "I can't be late. You work in the opposite direction than me."

Heather pouts at me.

"Fine. You can take my car, and I'll take my bike. Okay?"

Heather smiles. "Driving the Mercedes. Woohoo, lucky me."

"It's a car, Heather."

"Yes, a very expensive car. You know there's a correlation between how much you pay for a car and how big your—"

"Enough! And it's size, not price."

Heather laughs, and it causes me to grin at her. She's the youngest of all my siblings. Although she's a twin, Heather came last, and as a result, she has all of us wound around her little finger.

I walk into my bedroom, grab my jacket and briefcase, and head for the front door.

The keys to my car are on the hall table, so I pick them up and find Heather waiting for me outside.

"No speeding," I say as I jangle the keys in front of her.

"I'd never," replies Heather, holding her hand to her chest.

"Yeah, yeah, yeah. I mean it, Heather. I'm not taking another ticket for you."

"All right." Heather sighs and smirks at me. "I know you look GQ and all, but are you really going to wear your Versace suit on a bike?"

"It's Armani and yes. I have my leather jacket and helmet in the garage. Drive safely and have a good day. I'll see you tonight."

I pull her into me, kiss the top of her head, and walk toward the garage. Thankfully, I have my own office at work with a bathroom attached, so I can fix my hair when I get there. I need to look my best for the board meeting.

My car is parked in the driveway. I hear Heather open and close the door, and I turn to wave her goodbye. She's smiling at me, and I grin back at her. The car turns over once and makes a strange noise, then I'm flying through the air. Heat and debris engulf me, and I'm slammed into an oak tree. I get up, something drips into my eyes. It stings. I rub at them, look at my hand, and see blood. I stand, take a step, and fall onto my knees.

Heather.

I have to get to Heather.

I stand again, staring at the place where my car was. There's nothing there but a shell and flames.

I drop to my knees and scream, "Heather!"

Pushing up again, I take two steps, trip, and blackness engulfs me.

CHAPTER 1

Eric

The heat is blistering today. I'm underneath an old Mustang which needs more new parts than the owner can afford. So I've made do with some reconditioned parts and improvised as much as I can. He's made it clear to my boss, Theo, it's all he can afford no more than the bare minimum. He'd be better off selling it for parts and buying something else, but apparently, he's attached. I don't usually work on cars. I prefer bikes. And on a day like today, I'd give just about anything not to be stuck under this piece of crap soaking my overalls through with sweat.

"Yo, Eric! You finished with the 'stang yet?" asks Theo.

I slide out from under it and frown at him. "Am I still working on it?"

Theo holds up his hands to placate me. "The owner's here, what should I tell him?"

"That it needs a match and a nice funeral?"

"You're a grumpy fucker, aren't you?"

"Theo, it's not worth fixing. She's rusted in more than a few places. If he had the money, we could do it right, and she'd be a beauty, but he doesn't. She's a hazard, a fucking death trap." I stand and reach for a towel to drag over my face and wipe my hands.

"Yeah, yeah, I know, but he wants it fixed. Can you get it running?"

I sigh and nod. "Yeah, but not until later today or early tomorrow."

"That's the best you can do?"

I answer him with a death glare, and he backs away from me, arms raised.

It's easy work for me, it's what paid my way through school. It was never a passion working on cars, bikes, hell, any type of machinery. Not enough money in it. And if it's not a challenge, then what's the point? You should always push yourself to achieve the best, and it shouldn't come too easy.

I sit on a stool and open a bottle of water. The overalls I'm in are murder, so I undo them and free my upper body. It gives me a little relief from the heat, and the cold water is like liquid gold as it slides down my throat.

"Is this what you mean by working on my Mustang, Theo?" I turn to see a man in his late sixties staring at me disapprovingly.

"Mr. Lake, Eric's been working on it all morning. Even—"

The old geezer faces Theo and yells, "I need my damn car!"

I stand and walk toward him, and the old guy turns and eyes me warily. "Mr. Lake?" He nods. "Your car needs probably another three hours of work. I'm sure Theo has told you, it's a pile of crap. You'd be better off buying a newer car."

Mr. Lake's face goes bright red, and a vein in his neck begins to pulsate. "I don't want a newer car. I want—" He clutches his chest and goes down on one knee.

"Fuck! Theo, call an ambulance." I rush toward the older man and lay him down on the filthy garage floor. "Mr. Lake, I need you to breathe deeply."

Theo has his phone out and is talking to someone.

I stand and jog toward the first-aid kit, pulling it open, and take an aspirin out. I hold them up to Theo. "Tell them I'm giving him aspirin." Theo nods and relays the information. "Mr. Lake, are you on any heart medication? Have you experienced anything like this before?" He shakes his head. "This isn't going to taste very nice, but I need you to chew on these and try to stay calm. Breathe deeply and relax."

The old man nods, fear hiding in the depths of his eyes.

Theo comes toward us with a clean towel in his hands.

"I'm going to put this under your head." Mr. Lake nods. "Tell me about your car." I need to get the old guy's mind off his troubles.

Tears well in his eyes, and I'm unprepared for what he says. "It's for my granddaughter, Cherie." Mr. Lake clutches his chest. His speech becomes soft, and he's gasping for breath. "My son, her father, was a useless, spineless, excuse for a man. Cherie's had it hard her whole life. I want to do it up, to leave her something, so she'll know she was loved… by me, at least."

I nod, understanding how he feels. My parents did the best they could, but with five boys and one girl, it wasn't easy. We often went without.

I glance at the Mustang, rust eating away at her and look down at the old man as compassion washes over me. "I'll work on her. I'll find a way to bring her back to life."

"I don't expect you to do it for nothing." Fire still burns in the old guy, and he manages to sound annoyed even in his current state.

"Calm down. There will be a cost, but we'll figure it out." The old man closes his eyes, and I look up at Theo. "How far out are they?"

"They should be here any minute, it's a small town."

I nod and sigh. Population five thousand in Breckenridge, Colorado. I've never been one for small towns, and now I've been living here for three very long years. I keep to myself and live on the outskirts of town. The nearest neighbor to me is five miles away, and I have a gravel driveway, so I can hear if anyone comes calling. Not that anyone even knows where I am or if I'm alive. When I first moved here, I thought it would be a year, two tops.

The ambulance pulls in, and I move out of the way of the two paramedics as they run into the garage.

"He's in his late sixties, no previous heart condition. I laid him out and gave him two aspirin to chew on, and he's been responsive."

One of the paramedics looks at me. "Do you have medical training?"

"No, sir, I watch a lot of TV," I say, avoiding eye contact. "I'll get out of your way." Moving toward the front of the garage, I swipe my water bottle and stand outside away from questions and any possibility of them getting near the truth.

This town has an average temperature of seventy in summer, but this year we're having a heatwave—it must be one hundred and five. I can feel sweat as it trickles down my back. I watch as they load Mr. Lake into the ambulance.

Theo comes and stands near me. "You watch a lot of TV? You don't even own a TV."

I glance at Theo and smile. "What? You think I'd be working here if I were a doctor? Come on, Theo, I'm a dumb, ole mechanic, but a good one who's had enough for today and is going home. It's too hot to work."

"Yeah, okay," replies Theo suspiciously. "Don't forget Mrs. Dorthamer is dropping her car off for a service this afternoon. I told her it would be ready by lunchtime tomorrow."

I groan and look up at the clear blue sky. "I'll come back later and work on it in the cool of the night. It's supposed to be hotter tomorrow. I'm not working under a car in the one-hundred-degree heat."

Theo makes a noise, and I glance at him. He knows better than to push me as I'm the best mechanic he's got. I don't call in sick, I don't fraternize with the other staff, and I don't go out drinking all night and not come in the next day. He also pays the minimum wage, which is barely enough for a person to live on. I get a grand total of eleven dollars and ten cents per hour, and *if* I do overtime, he pays me sixteen dollars and sixty-five cents.

"I'll do the work, Theo, but not now or in the heat of the day."

"It's not that. I can't afford the overtime."

I quirk an eyebrow at him. Since I've been here, I know his business has doubled. I've even shown him where to invest his money to get a better return, and all he's worried about is paying me overtime.

"I'm not asking you to pay me overtime. I'll do my hours but at night. One of the reasons I moved here was for the climate. It's not supposed to get this hot."

Theo slaps me on the back. "Good man. Go home. Relax. And come back later. You still have keys, right?"

I'm also the only employee he trusts with keys to this place. "Yeah, I've got keys."

"Well, seeing as you're going to be here working, we might as well leave the lights on and see if anyone wants gas or drinks." The fucker is smiling at me. He sure likes a pound of flesh for his dollar.

"Sounds fair," I mumble as I go back inside the workshop and grab my helmet. "Have a good one. I'll be back when the heat breaks tonight. After today, I'll work nights, book whatever you want in."

Theo smiles, thinking he's had a win. I don't mind. This job is the only thing I have that keeps me sane.

CHAPTER 2

Eric

The ride home feels good against my skin. I take it slow and enjoy the freedom only being on a bike can bring. My home sits on the side of a mountain—one way in and one way out. If I get cornered up there, I can get out through the mountains—only an experienced hiker would be able to follow. I park my bike in the shed I built and walk toward the house.

I'm not used to living in snow country, and I should have positioned it closer to the house. Come winter, it's a pain to walk through sleet and snow to get inside. Rookie mistake. It's July, so I still have plenty of time to build a walkway between the two buildings, but as I ride a motorcycle, there seems little point in doing it. Although when I get snowed in, it would be nice to get wood from the shed without freezing to death. I keep a pile on the porch, but when it's cold, you burn through it quickly.

It's not much of a house—a bathroom, and the rest is an open plan. I picked it for the remote location, and if I wanted to extend it, I could. Apart from the shed, I've made no plans to expand.

Once inside, I strip off and stand under the shower, letting the cool water wash over my skin. I'm on well water. Normally, I'm quick, but today I stay in here until my skin goes pruney. As soon as I turn the water off, the oppressiveness of the heat washes over me. I grab a towel, wrap it around my hips, and walk into the kitchen. Too late, I realize someone is in my home as I smell the sickly scent of perfume.

"You know, it's an easy way to get yourself killed."

I freeze, analyzing the voice—female, not familiar, doesn't sound threatening. I keep a gun in my bedside table. I walk in that direction, drop my towel on the bed, open a drawer, pull out a pair of briefs and the gun at the same time. Turning around, I level the gun at her only to find an amused expression on her face, and her eyes staring at my crotch.

"Who the fuck are you?" I growl.

Slowly, her eyes move up my body, stopping briefly on the gun. The smile gets all soft and lazy as she holds up her credentials. "I'm Connor Styles' replacement, U.S. Marshal Maria Lovett at your service." Her eyes drop to my crotch again, and a small smile plays on her lips.

"You couldn't knock?"

"I did, you didn't answer, so I came *running* to your rescue."

I give her my back and put on my briefs, then open a cupboard and tug on some jeans.

"Why isn't Styles here himself to tell me he's being replaced?"

She doesn't answer, so I turn around. She's no longer staring at me but out the window. It takes her a moment before she visibly pulls herself together, looks at me, and gives a tight smile.

"I regret to inform you that U.S. Marshal Connor Styles was killed in the line of duty."

"Shit. I'm sorry. He was a tough old bastard." She nods and looks downhearted. "You need a drink?"

"Got anything cold?"

"Beer and water," I say as I walk away from my bed toward the fridge.

"Beer."

I'm surprised. Styles never once had anything but coffee or water. Definitely never alcohol. Placing my gun on the kitchen counter, I open the fridge and retrieve two beers. Twisting off the caps, I offer one to her.

"Are you here to tell me I'm free or to be the bearer of bad news?" I ask as I take a sip.

"The bearer of bad news, I'm afraid." She walks toward me, and I hand her the bottle.

"Maria?" She nods. "I've been here for three years. I want to go home. I miss my brothers, they think I'm dead." I look her in the eyes. "You need to talk to someone, let them know, I need this to end."

"Mr. MacKenny, you know as well as I do, you can't come in until you testify. Right now, they think you're dead, and you're safe. If you rise from the grave, you're putting your brothers in danger. I know you haven't forgotten your sister, Heather."

The mere mention of her name causes me physical pain. My sweet sister, Heather, who always looked to me to make things right. Heather, who's been dead for three years. My sister that I didn't protect. *Will my brothers ever forgive me if I come back?*

"I'm sorry, I didn't mean to cause you… that is, I didn't mean to…" says Maria in a softer tone.

"It's all right, Maria. It wasn't your fault. Let's face it, it was mine."

"Your sister's death wasn't your fault either. It was those scumbags at Zed Fluid Systems. You have to be patient." Maria sounds sympathetic, but I've been doing this long enough to know they'll say anything to get me to do what they want.

I walk toward the kitchen table, pull out a chair, and sit down. "I should have known better. How much longer do I have to wait?"

Maria takes a seat opposite me. "It's not so bad here, is it? You have a job, friends, a home."

"I'm doing a menial job, earning minimum wage, and I live in the middle of fucking nowhere. As for friends, I have no attachments. I'm not endangering anyone else."

"And if you go home, don't you think they'll go after your family? You have to be patient, we're working as fast as we can."

With one question about my family, I concede defeat. I will remain here, but I don't have to like it. "Fine." I sigh and scrub a hand over my face. "But I need more money."

"You said it yourself, you live in the middle of nowhere. What could you possibly want more money for?"

I lean forward across the table, pinning her with a look. "I have over fifteen million dollars in an investment account. It's my goddamn money, and I want access to it," I say with conviction.

"Mr. MacKenny... Maddock, you know we can't. We've frozen your accounts, even your brothers don't understand why and are continually serving us with legal documents to have it and all your assets released." Maria matches my gaze, sighs, and continues, "How much do you need?"

I haven't had anyone call me Maddock in three years, even U.S. Marshal Styles always called me Eric, so I wouldn't get confused.

"In this town, this hell-hole, my name is Eric, Eric Hill. I don't want you, God forbid, blowing my cover." Maria nods but looks bemused. "I need to fix up an old Mustang for a customer. He doesn't have the money to do it."

"Selfless, too? You really are the whole package, *aren't* you?"

Her words cause me to look at her and take her in. She's in her early thirties, trim with a short blonde hairstyle, not unattractive but not something I'd usually go for. My girlfriend, Regina, is probably married by now. I have a lot to make up for after so much time has been lost.

"I'm a bastard, Ms. Lovett. It's how I made my money, and it's how I ended up here." I raise my hands and look around the room, taking in my small mountain cabin which consists of one big open space. The only room with walls is the bathroom.

"Yeah, right. I can't swing you cash, but the American government confiscates cars every day from illegal activities. Write down the model and make, and I'll see if I can get you parts."

It's better than nothing. I feel like I've had a win and grin at her while lowering my hands. "Thank you."

She stands, placing her hand on her hip, exposing her gun and badge at the same time. Styles used to do that too, makes me wonder if they teach them to do it at marshal school.

"Keep safe, maybe install an alarm system that lets you know if anyone opens your front door? If I'd been one of Zed's hitmen, you'd be dead."

"I'm not normally home through the day," I reply as I stand.

"It's the little things that can get you killed. Only takes one person, Mad-Eric, to recognize you, then everyone you know is in danger," Maria says seriously as she heads toward the front door.

"Isn't it why you moved me across the country? No one I know would come here."

"Pays to be careful."

I nod at her, not wanting to argue. She opens the front door, waves at me, and
walks out. I follow her, and the heat hits me like a wall.

"Is it always this hot?"

"Nah, we're having a fucking heatwave. Drive careful U.S. Marshal Maria Lovett, the roads up here can be tricky."

She hands me her card. "I know you have all the regular numbers in case of an emergency, but if you need anything, you give me a call."

I walk to the edge of my porch as she continues to her car. Maria leans into the passenger window and comes out with a large yellow envelope. She walks it back to me, holding it out.

"This is why you're still dead. I thought you might like to see how your family is doing. The FBI keeps tabs on them. There are written reports on your brothers and photos. It might make it easier for you to stay here?" Maria smiles once more, then turns on her heel and goes to the car.

I'm holding the envelope in my hand. I don't even look up when she drives away. My brothers are inside—Kyle, Angus, Jamie, Sean, and Lochlan. Slowly, I walk back inside and place it on the dining table. I can't look at it right now. Instead, I move toward my bed, strip off my jeans, and lay down.

Kyle is the oldest and the smartest too. He's head of the Loyal Rebels MC. All of us have been affiliated with the club, but Kyle wanted more for us. Growing up, I worked in the garage fixing bikes and cars. I remember when I turned fifteen, Kyle was twenty-two, and told him I was going to drop out of school and work there fulltime. He beat me until I was bloody and told me I was smarter than that. Kyle wouldn't let me near the MC or the garage for three months. Told me I needed to find something else. He guided me, in his own way, toward accounting.

I did the books for the club for a long time until the day came when Kyle again told me I needed to move on. Kyle isn't ashamed of his club, fuck, he loves it. He kept telling me I could do better, and I did. Well, until my world fell apart.

Angus is a year younger than me. He went into computers, a complete nerd in. He works for himself, but he's into hacking for money. Angus is scary good. He can find out all about you from a thread of information. When they put me into witness protection, I warned them about him. Not his illegal activities, but that they could leave nothing for him to find.

Jamie is so unlike all of us, not one for big cities or lots of people. He owns a small farm where he grows fruit, vegetables, and free-range chickens. I had no idea how much money was involved in organic. I used to do his books too—the crazy prices people will pay for organic food is mind-boggling. If you get him started, he'll rave for hours about how insecticides are bad for you, and the hormones in meat will have you growing a second head.

Sean is the most like Kyle—he's street smart. He was always involved in fights at school, usually in defense of someone weaker than him. Sean abhors bullying and always defends the underdog. He went into the Marines after school but only stayed in for eight years. Said it was enough life experience for him. He came back different, harder. Sean is Kyle's VP and handles security for the club when they need it.

Lochlan was Heather's twin. He must have felt her loss more than any of us. Lochlan is good looking. We all look alike, but Loch has higher cheekbones and fuller lips. When I last saw him, he was trying to find himself, whatever the fuck that means. Loch has always used his looks to get by in life. He went into modeling, and I've seen his picture a few times in magazines since I've been trapped here. He's been smart. When I last checked, he was an ambassador for many high-profile brands. I suppose he's found his calling.

That's my family, the MacKenny clan. Our father was a proud Scottish man who drank too much and loved our ma too much. Dad and Ma were out one night. Both of them had too much to drink, and he drove into the path of a truck, killing both of them. It was our grandfather, Da, who looked after us from that day forward. He was a better man than our father. Family always came first. If you pick on one of us, you deal with all of us. Growing up, I always felt protected, loved, and part of something bigger. If I didn't have my brothers, I had the MC.

Holding up my arm, I look at the tattoo on my forearm. It's a take on the Victoria Cross. My grandfather received for his efforts in the Scottish military. It's a cross with a circle. Within it are the words, *In Memory of K.M.*, our grandfather, who taught us what family was all about—to love them no matter what—we don't all have to be the same, and we need to find our own paths, no matter where they may lead.

He was a tough old bastard, but he loved us, and when our parents died, Da stepped in. He didn't even think about it, he just did it. I always felt Kyle, being his namesake, made it his mission in life to guide us after Da died. Da would have been proud of him.

The tattoo is one of the things they wanted me to get rid of, but all of us boys have them. I wasn't giving it up. It keeps me tied mentally to my family, and when you've been away from them as long as I have, sometimes, it's all the comfort I have.

I close my eyes, thinking about family and the choices we all made and drift off to sleep where I dream of Heather, alive, and I am with them all again.

When I awaken, darkness has fallen, but the heat hasn't abated. I go into the bathroom, shower in the darkness, cooling off in the process. I emerge feeling refreshed. Flicking on a light, I find what I need to wear to go back to the garage and head into the kitchen. The coffee pot is ready to go, so I hit the switch, and my eyes catch on the yellow envelope.

I walk toward it, wanting to see but not wanting to know. They all continued without me, and although I want that, I also want to be a part of their lives, but I'm not. I'm here in the mountains far away from them.

I undo the clip and reach in, pulling out a wad of papers and pictures. Kyle is on top. He's sitting on his Harley at a set of lights, not smiling, looking determined. On the back is a woman with long blonde hair and not much else. He always did like the slutty-looking ones. The paperwork attached to the photograph gives me a rundown on his life. There's nothing there I didn't already know except that they seem to think the woman, Lola, is a permanent fixture in his life.

Next up is Sean. He's staring into the lens, giving them the bird. Clearly, he hasn't changed, except for more tattoos. He's the epitome of a biker—dark glasses, a bandanna around his head, and a beard. The report on him claims he's involved with illegal trafficking of guns, but as yet, they haven't proved it, and they won't. He's too smart for them. No one in our family has spent more than a night in jail, and that's the way it's going to stay. Not to say we don't bend the law, we do, but we don't get caught.

The next picture is of a man with a hoodie pulled over his face. He has gloves on, long sleeves, and jeans. It could be anyone, but the paperwork says it's Angus. I wish I could see his face better. Whatever Angus is thinking is always right there for the world to see. He's an open book—every emotion or thought process goes across his face. You can actually see his mind working by his expression. There are two written sentences about him. 'Computer specialist who works for himself. Possibly a hacker for hire but nothing can be proven.' That's it. I wish there were more.

Next comes Loch, with a photograph obviously taken at a professional shoot. He's staring into the camera, looking cocky and arrogant. A woman is clinging to him, and he has the barest of smiles on his lips—must be for some ad campaign. The file on him reads, 'International model currently in Italy. No ties or connections to the Loyal Rebels MC.' This whole sentence makes no sense to me. Kyle, his brother, is the President of the MC. You can't get more tied to the MC than that.

I put the pieces of paper and photographs on top of each other as I read through them. The last is Jamie. He's at a farmers' market. He's smiling as he holds out an apple to a customer. He looks happy, certainly more so than the rest of them. The paperwork reads, 'A farmer who rarely comes into contact with the other members of his family.' This I find hard to believe. Jamie is the one in the family who never forgets birthdays or special events. He's the recordkeeper.

I pull the photographs out of the pile and place the paperwork back in the envelope. I position them beside each other and stare at my family.

I've been gone too long.

I miss them.

Standing, I toss the envelope into a drawer, but I leave the pictures on the table. I glance at them one last time and then head into work.

CHAPTER 3

Eric

It's been three days since the old man, Mr. Lake, had his heart attack. I've been working nights, and today is my day off. The heat feels never-ending as I drag my sorry ass out of bed. Walking into the kitchen, I absently turn on the coffee maker and stare out the window to the valley below. I've never been one for the countryside—big cities are all I've ever known. I have to admit there is a soul-calming beauty to this place. The seclusion is enough to drive me insane, but if I had someone to share it with, I could settle here for a while. But the urge for the city and the pace of it will always be my first love.

The coffee maker clicks off, and I pour myself a cup and sit at my dining table, sipping it. The photographs are all still here, and although I don't get visitors, I should put them away. If a U.S. Marshal can walk in here unannounced, so could anyone else. Maybe she was right. I should put in some sort of alarm system.

My phone starts to buzz, and I pick it up. It's Theo. *Great.* I have two days off, and I'll be damned if I'm going into work today.

I hit 'answer' on the phone. "Yes."

"Eric?"

"Yes, Theo, it's me." Annoyance colors my tone.

"Eric, the Mustang, it has to go."

"We promised the old guy we'd take care of it. You have plenty of fucking room, so what's the problem?"

"I don't do charity work. If you want to work on this, you're going to have to do it on your own dime."

I pull the phone away from my ear and groan. I can hear his mumblings as I try and get myself together. The 'stang isn't in anyone's way. Theo wants the all mighty dollar, and I guess he knows the old dude doesn't have any.

I place the phone back to my ear. "… not that I'm not sympathetic to Mr. Lake, but if I do it for one—"

"All right! I'll take care of it today, even if I have to get it towed here. Will that satisfy you, Theo?"

"You know, Eric, you can be a surly fucker."

Fan-fucking-tastic. Theo is annoyed at *me*.

"Theo, I said I'd take care of it, and I will. Is that all?" I ask with irritation in my voice.

"Yes. One day you and I are going to have a sit-down and talk about your attitude," says Theo cockily.

I sigh. It's too fucking early in the morning to be butting heads with him. We both know how much money I bring in. He's not going to fire me, but from time to time, he finds it necessary to exert his supposed superiority over me.

"Not today, Theo, it's my weekend. See you later." I click off and drop the phone on the table. It falls next to Loch's picture. Sadness wells within me as I stare at my family. I remind myself it is for them that I keep away, for their safety. I gather the photographs and walk toward a cabinet of drawers. I open the top one, flick through them one last time and place my memories inside.

I go back to my coffee, finish it, and head for the shower.

It's ten o'clock by the time I finish the few chores I have around my house, and I've decided the best course of action is to see if Mr. Lake has room at his home for the Mustang. I could bring it out here, but my shed isn't big enough.

The trip into town doesn't take long. I pull in front of the hospital and walk through the doors toward the reception desk. My mind is elsewhere, and I walk straight into a courier, sending his parcels flying.

"Jesus! Man, I'm so sorry." I scramble to help him pick up his deliveries. "I had my mind on other things."

"It's all right. I guess if you're in a hospital, you have bigger things to worry about." He smiles at me with understanding on his face. I don't have the energy or the inclination to inform him otherwise, so I give him a nod.

As I hand him the last envelope, he gives me a strange look.

"Is everything okay?" I ask.

"My name's John."

"Eric," I say automatically.

"Thanks for helping me pick them up, Eric. You have a good day."

He gives me another quizzical look, then continues on his way. I watch him walk out of sight, and he doesn't look back. Shrugging, I head for the reception desk, paying more attention to my surroundings.

"May I help you?" asks an older woman from behind the desk.

"I'm looking for a friend, Mr. Lake."

"First name?" she asks.

"I don't know."

She sits back and assesses me. "He's your friend, but you don't know his *first name*?"

"I'm working on his car. My boss is about to have it towed to a wrecking yard. I was hoping to talk to Mr. Lake and see if I could drop it off at his home…" I pause, searching for the right words. "I'm trying to do something nice here," I say as an explanation and smile at her convincingly.

She looks at me shrewdly for a good ten seconds before she starts hitting the keyboard to find Mr. Lake.

"He's on the fifth floor, room 503. The elevators are behind me to the left."

"Thank you, I appreciate it."

She gives me the barest of smiles before she looks behind me to the next person.

I follow her directions and find Mr. Lake sitting up in bed glaring at a nurse while she speaks to him. He's hooked up to machines, and from the expression on his face, he's not happy. Mr. Lake's still an ornery old fucker.

He waits for her to finish, then he says, "I'm not a child. I am perfectly capable of looking after myself."

The nurse smiles sweetly at him and replies, "If that were the truth, Mr. Lake, you wouldn't be here now, would you?"

She turns on her pretty little heels and walks from the room, smiling broadly at me. I look at Mr. Lake, and his face is so red, I think he's ready to have another heart attack or a stroke.

"Hey, Mr. Lake. How are you feeling?" I ask.

"Suddenly, everyone thinks I'm incapable of looking after myself. I'm frustrated, the food stinks, and I want to go home. But does anybody care what I want? No." His outburst causes me to laugh.

I pull out a chair and sit down next to his bed. "Do you remember me?"

"I had a heart attack. I didn't lose any of my mental capabilities."

"Or your kind way of speaking, I see."

The old man squints his eyes at me and throws his hands in the air with frustration. "I apologize, it's been a bad few days." Although he's saying the right words, I can tell by his demeanor he's had enough of everything.

"You did suffer a major medical event."

Mr. Lake scoffs and looks at the ceiling. "I'm aware of that."

Laughter rumbles up out of my chest, and the old guy looks at me. "Sorry, but having a heart attack is a serious, and it can lead to memory loss. Clearly, this isn't the case with you."

"Not that I don't appreciate the visit, Eric, but what can I do for you?"

I like his directness—to the point, no small talk, no fuss.

"The owner of the garage, Theo, would like it if we moved your car. I'll still work on it. In fact, I have a buddy looking into getting me some parts, cheap, but we need to move it."

He frowns at me. "I thought you said it would be fine at the garage."

"Things change. Is there room at your home? Do you have a garage or work shed? Something big enough for me to work on it?" I have no intention of explaining to Mr. Lake about my boss, Theo, and how he is a money-hungry asshole who is only looking out for himself.

"I have a barn. It's big enough. You sure you don't mind working on it?"

"Nope. It'll be a pleasant distraction on my days off and after work if I don't have anything going on."

"You don't have a wife, a girlfriend or a... partner?" asks Mr. Lake.

His subtle attempt to find out my sexual preference makes me laugh louder than before, and soon he joins in too.

"No, Mr. Lake, I don't have a wife or a girlfriend. Too busy with work," I say, grinning at him.

"Let me get this straight. You're good-looking, single, you have a job, and no female in this tiny town is interested in you? You sure you're *not* gay?"

More laughter erupts from me. "No, sir, I'm *not* gay. My life is complicated. I don't think it'd be fair to bring a woman into it."

He eyes me suspiciously, frowns, and says, "Okay. Do you know the big red barn out by Little Creek Road?" I nod. "It's my place. You can put it in the barn and work on it from there if you like. But I still want to pay you."

"Don't worry about that, Mr. Lake. We'll work something out."

"Yes, we *will*. My granddaughter, Cherie, is out there from time-to-time feeding my animals, but the barn is never locked. Help yourself to it."

I stand, extend my hand to him, and he grasps mine in his. There's strength still in those old bones. "Sounds like a plan. How long are they keeping you?"

"I'm sure they are trying to wring me for every last dollar I have. I don't know. The goddammed doctor wants to keep me in for further observation, so until he gives me the all-clear, I'm stuck."

I chuckle. "I'm sure it's for the best."

"Pfft... bloodsuckers!" I grin at him, shake my head, and walk toward the door. "Wait!" I turn around and raise an eyebrow at him. "Could you muck out the horses and check on my chickens while you're out there... please?"

Spark

Mr. Lake looks uncomfortable. He's avoiding eye-contact. It must be hard to suddenly have to ask for help as pride often gets in the way.

"I can do that, but you'll owe me."

"Son, there's only so much I can afford," he admits, and all the fire goes out of him.

"I like eggs, do your chickens lay?"

"Yes," he says, looking at me once more.

"Good. Is it cool if I take some eggs every now and then?"

"Absolutely! Best eggs in the county," Mr. Lake says proudly.

"Okay, and when you get out of here, I'm thinking you can make me lunch on Sundays."

His fire comes back. "Won't be a roast every Sunday, you know."

"I didn't ask for a roast. I asked for lunch, don't care what it is, so long as I don't have to cook or prepare it. Fair?"

The old guy smiles at me and nods. I nod back and walk out of the room. As I pass the nurses station, I stop and talk to the nurse who was in his room.

"He doing okay?" I ask, gesturing toward Mr. Lake's room.

"He'll be fine. This was a wake-up call. He can't be looking after his farm and doing all the things a much younger man should be doing. Mr. Lake needs to learn how to slow down," says the nurse.

I nod, purse my lips, and head toward the exit. How does an old man with only a granddaughter slow down? It's obvious he doesn't have a lot of money, and this hospital stay will probably break the bank if he doesn't have health insurance.

CHAPTER 4

Eric

A week later, and I'm in Mr. Lakes' barn under the Mustang. The old man is still in the hospital, which makes me think there's more wrong with him than he'll admit. His chickens produce more eggs than any one person could possibly eat, so I bought an old wooden desk and made a roof to go over it with a sign saying, 'Eggs for Sale, Two Dollars a Dozen.'

I placed it at his front gate, left some eggs out, and I check on it every afternoon. The eggs sell, and so far, the honor system appears to be working. I don't know what one old guy was doing with all those eggs, but at least now, he's making some money.

Today is Sunday, and the heat finally feels like it's breaking. There's a cool breeze, and I'm working in my overalls with a white T-shirt underneath. I have Metallica blaring on the portable stereo and am singing 'Enter Sandman' at top of my lungs.

The parts from the U.S. Marshal turned up in the shape of a whole goddamn car. It feels criminal to strip it, but I can't give the old guy a mint Mustang. He'd know I was into something shady. So, I've been taking what I need and fitting it to his car.

I'm engrossed in my work, singing, when someone kicks my boot.

"Hello?" I yell out.

I look to my left, and I see tan boots with pink fancy-work on them, walking away, then my music stops.

"Hello?" I repeat.

"Who the hell are you?"

Whoever she is, she's pissed. She's even tapping one foot. I roll out and look up at the cutest female I've seen in a while, and she's all kinds of angry. Her foot is still tapping, hands on her hips, and she's looking down at me with a serious amount of attitude on her face. My eyes travel up her body from her boots to her short skirt, to the way-too-tight tank top, and finally, I lock eyes with her.

"You first," I say with a grin.

"I beg your pardon?" she asks, shaking her head at me causing her ponytail to move from side to side.

"Who are you?" I ask teasingly.

"No, no, and *hell* no! *This* is my granddaddy's place. Who the hell are *you*?"

"Oh, so you're Cherie." I stand and extend my hand.

She looks me up and down, hands still on hips. "How do you know my name?"

I grin at her. "Your grandfather told me about you. Said you'd be here from time to time feeding animals and stuff. I've been coming out every day and haven't seen you once."

"So, you're the one who's been feeding the animals?"

"Yes, ma'am. I'm not a country boy, so I hope I've been doing okay. So far, they haven't complained," I reply with a wolfish grin.

"You. Still. *Haven't.* Told. Me. Your. Name." Cherie pauses between each word, exasperation evident in her tone.

I extend my hand again. "Eric Hill, Mr. Lakes' mechanic, and part-time ranch hand."

She grasps my hand and tries to squeeze it tightly. It's cute as hell. To let her know I'm more than capable of handling her, I squeeze back, not with my full strength but enough to let her know I'm stronger. Cherie gasps, and I release her. I like the sound, and I'm wondering what noises she'd make, naked and underneath me.

"How did my granddaddy convince you to do all this?"

"He dropped the Mustang off to get fixed, and that was where he had his heart attack." Cherie nods. "The owner of the garage wouldn't let me keep working on the 'stang there. So, your granddad suggested I work on it out here and wrangled me into looking after a few things."

"So, it was *you* who put up the stall out front?"

"Yes, ma'am. He told me I could have the eggs, but there are too many for one person, so I take what I need and sell the rest."

Her face clouds over. She looks me up and down and not in a good way.

"Oh, really? So, you thought you'd rip off a sick old man, did you?"

It's my turn to place my hands on my hips. I'm a good foot taller than her, and I lean over. "Lady, I don't know what male turned you into such a distrustful piece of work, but I don't operate that way. Mr. Lake asked me to help out. You think on my days off, and after work, I want to be taking care of animals *and* working on a car to be paid in eggs? The money for the eggs is in the jar behind you on the shelf. Have a nice fucking day," I reply icily as I stalk away.

Too much *trouble*.

She's been burned and good.

I don't need the aggravation or stress. *What was I thinking getting involved with the old guy?* He's going to be another person I disappear from when my time here is up.

I'm so angry I don't realize she's talking to me until I get to my bike, and she grabs my arm. I whirl on her, and she stumbles backward.

"I'm sorry. I knew someone was feeding and looking out for the animals, I didn't know who. I misjudged you, and I shouldn't have. You're right, I've been screwed over in the past, and it colors the way I look at the world, but I shouldn't have been so quick to label you." Her face is flushed, and she's talking quickly. She looks upset, and my instinct is to make her feel better.

I run a hand through my hair and look up at the sky. "I'm sorry, too. I shouldn't have said what I said. I'm out of practice with… women. Actually, people in general." I look down, her pretty little mouth is slightly open, and she looks surprised. "What?"

"*You're* out of practice with women? *You*?" Cherie asks. A blush creeps up her throat and colors her face.

I grin at her and nod. "Yeah, I don't know too many people here apart from the guys I work with, but I don't socialize with them."

"How long have you lived in Breckenridge?"

"Three years."

"You've lived here three years, and you don't have any friends? Male *or* female?" she asks disbelievingly.

I unzip my overalls to the waist and strip off the top part of them, revealing my white T-shirt and arms. Cherie's face goes a deeper red, and she looks quickly away.

"I don't socialize. I guess I like the quiet life," I say as I grin at her.

"That's umm… weird for someone like you," she replies.

"Someone like me? As in a mechanic slash ranch hand?" I ask cheekily.

Cherie looks up at me. "No, as in single and hot—"

"You think I'm hot?" I ask as I lean against my bike.

"I have to go. Nice meeting you. Thank you for looking after Granddaddy's farm and for selling the eggs." She turns around, stumbles, and walks quickly toward the barn.

I sit on my bike watching her ass in the mini skirt as she hurries away from me. It's been a while since a woman has caught my attention. This one seems like too much trouble, but my dick thinks differently as it twitches in its confines. It's nice to know she thinks I'm hot.

I start the bike, ride up to the barn, honk my horn, and do a two-fingered wave at her.

Spark

Cherie waves frantically at me, so I stop.

She comes running over. "Do you eat pizza and drink beer?"

"I've been known to try them on occasion."

"Well, as a thank you for looking after things, would you like to meet at The Roadhouse on the outskirts of town at say seven-ish?"

"Pizza *and* beer?"

Cherie places one hand on her hip, squares her shoulders, and says, "Yeah, and you can buy the beer."

I laugh at her, and her eyes go to my throat. "Sounds good. Want me to pick you up?"

Slowly, she drags her eyes up to meet mine. "No, I think I need to have my own way of getting home."

I wink at her. "Hmm, okay. See you then."

I ride out of the farm feeling happier than I have in years. On the way out, I pass an old truck which must be hers, and I wonder if it's been serviced in a while. Much like the Mustang, it needs a bit of tender loving care. Come to think of it, maybe it's what we all need.

Chapter 5

Cherie

Could I have made a bigger dork of myself than the way I acted with Eric? The man is a walking advertisement for sex. He must be six foot six with shoulder-length dark hair that you could hang onto while having the ride of your life. And those arms.

He's everything I like in a man. Which means he's *wrong.*

Granddaddy said I have the worst taste in men, and he's right.

The last one said he loved me, and I believed him, even when he said there were no jobs available, and I supported him for six very long months. I came home early one night from my waitressing job to find him having sex with my best friend.

Can you believe it?

I can't even choose my friends properly, and it made no sense. Tracey and I had been friends since before school. I would *never* have done anything so horrible to her. I followed her to Nashville while she chased her dreams of making it big as a country singer. I loved her, I helped her, and she betrayed me.

Not that I should be surprised. Most of the men I've dated over the years have been losers. I read somewhere once that we subconsciously date our fathers. Mine was a loser who either stole or lied his way through life. Dad ended up dead with a needle sticking out of his arm. My mother was only interested in his stuff so she could sell it and move out of town. I was fifteen. Tracey helped me through all of it, and her betrayal cut me to the core.

After I found Tracey and my ex together, I moved back home. The home I never wanted to come back to. Too many bad memories of useless parents. I truly believe some people should have to get a license to have a child. If it weren't for my grandfather, I wouldn't have come back, but then I wouldn't have had somewhere to run *to.* Don't misunderstand me, he's a lovable old, cranky pants, but he's not getting any younger, and he won't listen to me. I want him to sell the farm and buy something a little closer to town, maybe in a retirement village?

Granddaddy will have no part in it. Says when he dies, it'll be on his own two feet on the land he loves. I think the land he loves is plotting to kill him. He told me I will get everything when he's gone, which includes all the back taxes he owes. I'll have to sell everything to pay for them.

Sighing, I run a hand through my hair. I've taken it out of the ponytail, washed it, and lightly dried it. It's a little too long right now, falling below my shoulder blades. When I work, it either has to be up or in a hair net. The hair net makes me feel old. I'm only twenty-two. I feel like my bones are stretched thin, and my skin is pulled tight, giving me a grotesque appearance when I wear that thing. So, I try to wear my hair down as much as possible away from work. I have to wear flats when I'm working, but my feet still ache at the end of my shift. I don't want to be a waitress forever. I like looking after people and always wanted to go into social work. Granddaddy says it's my bleeding heart, maybe. I like to think if I survived my childhood, I could help others in a similar situation, perhaps help them find their way to the right path.

I don't wear a lot of makeup, but tonight I go to extra lengths to make myself look good. I have on a neutral shade of eyeshadow which makes my eyes pop. I've curled my lashes, and I've applied a nice, thick layer of mascara to make them look fuller than they are along with a little blush and bright red

Spark

lipstick. As I appraise myself in the mirror and smile. I look great. It's been ages since I've gone to this much trouble.

Walking back into my bedroom, I pick up my Miss Me jeans with the glittery studs on the back pockets and slip them on. I'm wearing my favorite black, lacy, push-up bra, and I need to pick a top which will show off my assets. My wardrobe consists of black, black, and more black. I find the perfect top—it's a crop top that crosses over with long sleeves and a cut-out up high which shows off a bit of cleavage. It screams sexy, and when I look at myself in the mirror, it's kind of trashy, but it's my style. I prefer the term country chic, but it's yet to catch on.

The only thing left to do is find a nice pair of shoes. My eyes go to the spiky gold-heeled black boots with the gold rose on the side. They are way too tall for me, and my feet already hurt, but they'll look killer with this outfit. I've also never worn them before. I paid way too much for them and have been waiting for a special occasion to wear them. The Roadhouse *isn't* a special occasion kind of place, but Eric *is*.

There I go again. I will *not* get involved with this man. I will be nice to him, I will buy him dinner, and I will say goodnight at the end of the evening, leaving him *alone*.

I smile at myself in the mirror, grab a little black bag, and head for the door.

When I enter The Roadhouse, the band is in full swing, and the place is packed. I make my way to the bar and order two beers, one for me and one for Eric *if* I can find him. The skin on the back of my neck rises, and I turn around to see Gil Weston leering at me.

Ugh! We went on three dates before I realized what a douche canoe he is. *See,* bad taste in men.

"Hello, Cherie… you're looking *mighty* fine this evening." It's barely seven, and he's already had too much to drink. His eyes travel over my body and stop at my boobs where the ass licks his lips.

"Hello, Gil," I reply with as much disinterest as I can muster.

"Here, let me get that for you," he says as he shoves a twenty at the bartender and brushes my chest along the way.

"No. I'm meeting someone. It wouldn't be right," I explain as I fish a note out of my ridiculously small handbag and hand it over.

"What? You're here with someone else?" asks Gil, a little too loudly, and people are beginning to stare.

Spark

I give him a tight smile and am about to respond when I feel an arm go around my waist. I look up, and it's Eric, giving Gil a death stare. "Hey, honey, you're running late. Did you already pay for these?"

I nod, mesmerized by his green eyes, and a tight-fitting black shirt that has enough buttons undone so you can get a glimpse of his chest.

He grabs the beers with his other hand, moving Gil out of the way and guides me to a booth in the back. "Who was that?" he growls as he sits beside me.

"*That* was three dates I'll never have back. That was a huge mistake. He still believes I like him. *That* was Gil West."

Laughter rumbles up and out of his chest, and I find myself staring at it. I like the way he laughs. It's full-bodied and sexy as hell.

"I was supposed to pay for the beer."

"What?"

"You said you'd pay for pizza and I'd buy the beer. It looks like the tables have turned, which is good as I've read their menu. I want a steak. You can have a pizza if you want or anything else that pleases you. My treat."

"No, that wasn't the deal. I'm supposed to buy *you* dinner, not the other way around."

"Honey, you were never going to buy me dinner, and I'm a little pissed you bought the beers. A gentleman doesn't let his woman pay for anything."

Oh, dear Lord, I like the way he sounds. But I am *not* going home with him.

I am not going home with him, I mentally chant a few more times in my head.

"Well, I'm not *your* woman, and this is a business transaction. I'm simply thanking you for looking after Granddaddy's farm and car."

Eric drapes an arm behind me on the booth, twists in his seat to look at me, and says, "Maybe I can think of other ways for you to thank me."

I swear to God my thighs light up, heat pools between my legs, and my mouth falls open.

I am not going home with him.
I am not going home with him.
I am not going home with him.

I keep repeating this on a loop in my brain, trying to get my mouth to work.

Eric chuckles and leans in. I look down at his mouth, wanting him to kiss me so badly. His lips are so close to mine, I can feel his hot breath on me. I'm about to close the gap when he says, "So, Cherie, do you still want..." he licks his lips, "... pizza?" He raises an eyebrow.

Fucker! He's toying with me. Fuck, fuck, fuckity fuck! He can obviously see I like him.

"No, I want the ribs, a side of mash potatoes, and dessert."

Spark

Eric throws his head back and laughs. "I like a woman who knows what she wants. You sure a little thing like you can eat all that?"

"Well, big guy, if I can't, I'm sure you can finish it off," I say with irritation.

"Oh, honey, you have no idea," he says seductively.

Bristling with frustration and a little embarrassed, I lean into him and say, "Oh, honey, it's you that has *no* idea."

For a moment, he holds his breath, his hand grabs the back of my neck, and I'm sure he's about to kiss me when the waitress slaps the table. "What'll it be?" she asks without looking at us.

I turn my head and say, "Whole rack of ribs and mashed potatoes."

Eric growls and looks up at her. "Your timing is impeccable. The largest steak you've got, medium rare, a side of fries, and that's it for now."

"Okay, I'm on it." She smiles at us and walks quickly away.

I'm facing the empty booth opposite me as Eric's fingers stroke my neck. My whole body is concentrating on the sensation and what he's doing to me.

"Cherie, look at me."

"I would if you'd sit opposite me. Don't you think it'd make conversation a bit easier?"

"If I sit opposite you, I can't touch you. Don't you want me to touch you?" Eric whispers sexily.

His other hand has moved to my knee, and I think I'm either about to explode or moan like a lovesick teenager.

"No. Actually, I don't," I say tersely.

His reaction is swift—he stands and sits opposite me. I'm overwhelmed with the feeling of loss from his touch.

"Okay, is this better? Sorry, I thought you liked it. It won't happen again," he says with a smirk like he knows what he's doing to me.

I smile at him. "Much better. Now, tell me about your job? Do you like it?"

I am so not listening to anything he's saying. *What is wrong with me?* I like him, big deal. It's not like we are going to get married and live happily ever after. *Why shouldn't I have some fun?* It's been nearly a year since John, and apart from my horrible dates with Gil, I've not even been in the company of a man. Gil and I didn't let get past first base. It turns out he's a nasty drunk, and I don't need that.

"Cherie? Cherie? Hello, is anyone home?" asks Eric staring at me.

"Sorry. It's been a big week. You've been nothing but kind to my grandfather and me. My feet are killing me, and I'm wearing these ridiculous shoes. You ever have a week where everything goes wrong?" My brain didn't filter one thing that came out of my mouth.

For a moment, he looks at me astonished and then laughs. I smile at him.

"Take off your boots," he orders.

"What?" I ask, confused.

"No one can see, take them off. If you want to dance later, we can put them back on, but for now, take them off."

"No, it's okay."

He runs a hand over his face. "Cherie, either you take off your boots, or I'll crawl under the table and do it for you."

Stricken with fear, I reach down and unzip my boots, pulling my sore feet free.

"Now, give me one of your feet."

"I will not," I hiss at him.

"You will do it now, or I'll cause a scene," he replies cockily.

Reluctantly, I raise my foot. He grabs it and rests it between his legs, then he begins to massage it.

Oh. My. God.

Heaven!

The closest I've come to a man massaging my feet is my foot massager my granddaddy got me for Christmas last year. I swear I've nearly worn it out, but *this*, this is so much better.

"This feels wonderful," I purr.

Eric chuckles. "Why did you wear those high heels? Don't get me wrong, honey, they are hot as hell. But if you've got sore feet, why wear them?"

"They're new. I've been waiting for a special occasion, and well, I figured The Roadhouse was as special as it was going to get," I reply honestly.

A look crosses his face. "So, this is a special occasion?"

"For a small-town girl with no prospects who works as a waitress, yes."

"Honey, I don't want you to wear those shoes again. Not until I take you somewhere worthy of them. I don't care what you have on your feet so long as you're comfortable, do you get me?"

It sounds like a command or order, but it doesn't feel that way. It feels like he wants to take care of me, but men don't do that to me. Men use me and move on. I nod my head as I mentally chant my mantra over and over again.

"I can see you *don't* get me, but you will. Where do you work?" he asks as he continues to work on my foot.

"The diner at the end of Main Street opposite the post office. Larry's Place."

"I've never been in there, but I think it's time I started ordering my lunch from there." He smiles and continues, "What days do you work?"

"I work Friday to Tuesday and get Wednesday and Thursday off."

"So, tomorrow's a day off?"

"Yeah, thank the Lord."

"You know my boss owes me a day. I could take you out for lunch, and you could show me the sights of Breckenridge." He grins at me while he's massaging my foot, and he's buying me dinner. Everything inside me screams, yes. He has the most amazing green eyes, and when he smiles, his whole face lights up. My head, on its own accord, nods in agreement, and his smile gets bigger.

"Good. So, tell me, where's good for lunch?"

I'm completely relaxed. He's managed to make me feel comfortable like I've known him forever.

"Would you mind if we went to Frisco? I don't need my boss getting upset if I frequent another restaurant. It's a small town, you know?"

"Give me your other foot." I immediately swap feet, and he starts working on it. "I get it, my boss, Theo, can be a dick."

I smile at him, and he grins back. "Have you explored the caves up near the ridge on the other side of town?"

"To be honest, Cherie, I've lived here for three years and haven't done a lot of exploring. I added a shed for my bike, I do some hiking around my home, and I work. That's about it." His face looks thoughtful as he mulls over what he's said to me. "I haven't been living, I've been existing. Maybe, I've punished myself for long enough."

"What does that mean?" I ask.

Eric shakes his head, grins, and says, "Nothing. Ignore me. I'm thinking about the past and not the future. Time to stop doing it. Would you like to go on my bike tomorrow?"

"Nice evasion there, Eric. You know part of getting to know someone is sharing. For instance, I don't like living in this town, too many bad memories."

"What kind of bad memories?" Eric asks.

"See what I did there? I shared something, and you want to know more, but no, I'm not going to elaborate until you do," I say smugly at him.

Laughter rumbles up out of his chest, and he nods at me. "Touché!"

The waitress returns and places our orders down in front of us. "Can I get you anything else?"

"Yeah, do you want another beer?" Eric asks me.

"Sounds good."

"Could we please get two Shiner Bocks?"

"On it," replies the waitress as she hurries off.

"Shiner Bock?" I ask.

"Sorry, didn't like the crap you got. Shiner Bock tastes better, trust me."

Self-confidence oozes out of him. Of course, I like Shiner Bock, but when you make next to nothing and are relying on tips to get you through the day, the cheaper beer will always do.

"I like Shiner Bock just fine."

Spark

"Another thing we have in common." He releases my foot, and I place it on the floor. "Going to wash my hands. Be back in a minute."

I smile at him and watch as he walks through the crowd. Most of them instinctively get out of his way. He's a big guy, and more than one female is looking at him longingly. I pick up my knife and cut my ribs into sections when Gil drops down beside me.

"Damn, girl. You gonna eat all that by yourself? You sure you don't need Gil to help you out?" Gil throws an arm over my shoulders and smiles at me leeringly.

"Gil, I'm on a date with my *man*. You should leave."

"Aww, don't be like that, Cherie. You know you like me," says Gil as his other hand moves to my knee.

I freeze, pin him with a look, and say, "Get your goddamn hands off me and leave me the hell alone."

Gil's face turns hard, he squeezes my knee and leans in. "You're a fucking waitress, and you've always thought you were too good for me. Well, I've got news for you, honey, you're not. You're trash. Just like the rest of your fam—"

Suddenly, Gil isn't next to me anymore. I look up, and Eric has him by the collar of his shirt and is frog-marching him through the bar and toward the front of the building. I stand and follow them out, without my shoes. Eric throws him to the ground, and Gil gets up, anger reverberating off him in waves.

"Stay down or walk away, those are your options," says Eric with a steel edge to his voice.

"Fuck you!"

"Buddy, you're drunk, and I'm not. It's simple physics. You come at me, you're going to get hurt, and trust me when I tell you, I'll fucking hurt you, and I'll enjoy it."

Gil looks up at me and smirks then looks back at Eric. "You know she's not worth it? She's the town bike. You know, everyone has had a ride." Gil spreads his arms wide, smiling at the gathering crowd.

All eyes come to me, and I am mortified. I can feel the color drain from my face.

Eric smiles and shakes his head. "Ahh, now I get it. She's the town bike, and everyone has had a ride... except you? That would mean the lady has taste. Which also means she's probably *not* the town bike, and even if she were, she probably still wouldn't fuck *you*."

Gil growls and charges Eric, who moves out of the way and kicks Gil in the ass as he goes past, sending him sprawling into the dirt. Gil stands, brushes himself off, and glares at Eric. "She's not fucking worth it!" Gil says, spraying spittle from his lips.

"Clearly, she is, or you wouldn't be making such a fuss," replies Eric.

Gil takes a step toward him, and Eric closes the gap with his fist aimed at Gil's jaw. He goes down and is out cold. A few of the locals clap and slowly disperse back into the bar, leaving me standing there, with no shoes, wanting the earth to open up and swallow me.

Eric looks up at me, but I can't read his face. I don't know what to say. I'm no virgin, but I'm not the town bike either. I can't get my voice to work, my mind is racing, and there's one clear thought traveling through it, *I need to leave.*

"Cherie, let's—"

"I want to go home. Would you mind going back in there to get my shoes and bag?" The words spill out of my mouth in a hurried succession.

"Cherie, we—"

"Really, I want to leave," I reply before he can say anything more.

Eric nods, goes back inside, and I walk on tiptoes over the stony ground toward my car, trying my best not to step on anything. It must be fifteen minutes before he re-emerges. I'm sitting on the hood of my car waiting impatiently. He walks out and has two brown paper bags, my shoes, and my handbag in his hands. I wave at him to gain his attention, and he makes his way to me across the parking lot.

When he reaches me, he drops to his knees, dusts off my feet, and places my shoes on them. I'm at a lost for words. He's defended my honor, and now he's like Prince-fucking-Charming putting the shoes on Cinderella, but this is no fairy tale—this is my shitty life.

Eric stands, dragging his hands up my legs as he positions himself between them. Heat pools in my core, and I gaze into his eyes.

He leans in, his mouth a hair's breadth away from mine and whispers, "I got our food to go. Do you want to come back to my place to eat it or at yours?"

I lean back. He grins at me, and right there, I know I'm in trouble. I know if I go home with him or he with me, I'll be having sex with him. This one is too good to be true, and I've had enough of knights in shining armor that start to rust as soon as life gets tough.

I take a deep breath, letting it out slowly. "I think I've had enough for one night. Raincheck?"

He stumbles back, looking surprised. "Ahh, okay. You know he's a dick? I make my own judgments on people. I don't listen to guys who can't take no for an answer."

I hop down off the hood, bend over, and pick up my bag next to one of the brown paper bags. "I know he's a dick. It's been a shitty day, and he's capped it off. I'm afraid I won't be very good company." I'm avoiding his eyes and searching through my tiny bag for my car keys.

"Cherie," says Eric. I find my keys and turn to open my car door. "Cherie," repeats Eric in a stronger tone. I look up at him. "Don't let this be how our night ends. Let me follow you home, we'll eat, talk, and I'll go home. No strings, no assumptions, just two people getting to know each other."

I quirk an eyebrow at him, and again, my head nods. He smiles, it's infectious, and I smile back.

"Okay, think you can keep up?" I ask.

"With your truck? Ahh, yeah… when was the last time it was worked on? When Christ was crucified?"

"Funny! I'll have you know she runs fine."

Eric quirks an eyebrow at me, bends over, and picks up the bags. "I'll take your word for it. Could you take these? It's a little hard on the bike."

"Yes. In case you lose me—"

"I won't," he replies with a smirk.

I huff at him, open my car door, and start my car. Eric turns and walks toward his bike.

I watch him go, liking the way he moves—confident, tall, and so sexy. Mentally, I berate myself, put my car in drive, and head for home.

CHAPTER 6

Eric

I swear she's driving it like she stole it. Either that or she's deliberately trying to lose me. It's not like there's a lot of traffic, so keeping up with her is easy, but in her piece of crap, she should be taking more care.

When Cherie pulls up in front of her home, she opens her car door and runs inside her house, leaving the food in her truck. I park behind her, climb off my bike, reach in and grab the brown paper bags, close the car door, and walk toward the front door.

She appears in the doorway. "Wait! Wait there," Cherie says as she closes the door on me.

This woman is too much trouble. I like her—she's hot, she's feisty, and she comes with more baggage than I can carry. I look around at her home.

It's on the fringe of town, the grass is overgrown, and the front screen door needs to have the hinges tightened and oiled.

The door flies open with a creaky groan, her face is flushed, and she's breathing hard. "Sorry, I wasn't expecting company, so I needed to clean up a bit," explains Cherie with a frown. I grin at her and hold up the bags. She moves to one side and ushers me in.

"You know your screen door needs some work."

"Hell, everything in here needs some work. But it's cheap, and the landlord leaves me alone, so long as I pay the rent on time."

"Do you often miss paying the rent?" I ask as I walk toward her dining table.

"Not anymore. Not now that I have regular customers and get paid on time. When I first moved back to town, it was a bit hit and miss." Cherie looks at the floor, then points to the kitchen. "Do you want me to reheat the food?"

"Cherie?" Her eyes come back to me. "You don't need to clean up for me. You don't need to explain anything to me. And yes, I want to use your microwave."

"I don't own a microwave."

I laugh and shake my head. "Who *doesn't* own a microwave?"

"Do you have any idea what they do to your food? So, no, no microwave, but I do have an oven.

It'll take a little longer, but I have beer, and we could talk while we wait."

Unbelievingly, I stare at her. She shuffles from foot to foot, and I can't tell if it's my gaze that's making her uncomfortable or having me in her home.

"Do you want me to leave?"

"No," Cherie replies quickly.

"You sure? Seems like I'm making you uneasy, and I don't want that."

"It's not you. I'm embarrassed about my home, The Roadhouse, Gil, and you had the foresight to think to go back in and grab the food. I was too wrapped up in my own mortification to think about anything or anyone but myself."

"Cher—"

Cherie holds up a hand. "Let me finish. Tomorrow is housework day. Through the week, I let my clothes fall where they want, and I do all my washing either tomorrow or the next on my days off. Gil and I went out on three dates. I didn't sleep with him as he's a fuckwad. I'm not the town bike, but I'm not pure as the driven snow either."

I can't help it. I laugh as her face goes bright red. I walk over to her, put my hands on her shoulders, look into her eyes only to receive a death stare, the anger's rolling off her in waves.

"Pure as the driven snow? Gil is a douche, your home is clean, and I don't care if you've left your clothes on the floor, it's *your* home. Don't be embarrassed. I'm starving. A beer and conversation sound good. So, calm down, I'm not laughing at you but with you."

"I'm not laughing," replies Cherie with a deadpan stare.

"True, but I haven't used my best lines on you yet." I grin at her, drop my hands, and walk into her kitchen, opening the oven door. "So you know, I have a microwave, but I won't put any of your food in it when you come to visit."

I take the food out of the bags and place it in the oven. When I turn around, her eyes are glued to my crotch. Quickly, she looks me in the eyes as a blush creeps up her neck.

"There's beer in the fridge." Cherie points at the refrigerator.

I open the door, grab two, and hand her one. "Do you want to sit at the table?"

"Sure, the table is fine."

I don't like it as she's avoiding eye contact, and I'm beginning to think I should leave.

"So, you've lived here for three years?"

"Yeah," I reply as I take a swig of my beer and pull out a chair. "You?"

A small smile plays on her lips. "I was born here. I left for a while, but you always return to what's familiar, you know?"

I understand what she's saying. If my brother, Kyle, hadn't made me leave the club, I'd still be there. Then again, if that had happened, I wouldn't be here.

I smile. "Yeah, I get it." I push up the sleeves of my shirt. "The familiar is comforting."

Her eyes are on my arm and the tattoo there. "What does it mean?" Cherie's fingers lightly trace the outline sending warmth through me.

"It's a family thing."

"*In memory of K.M.*, who's that?"

"Someone we all admired. It's a way to pay homage to him. He was a great man." I smile at her and ask, "How about you, any tattoos? I can't see any."

She giggles. "No, no tattoos for me. I've thought about getting one, but it's as far as I've gotten."

I like her laugh, and she finally seems to be relaxing. "Tell me about you. Do you like living back here?"

"It has its moments. I like being close to my granddaddy. He wanted me to live with him when I first got back, but I needed to stand on my own. I love it during ski season." Her whole face has lit up.

"I've never skied. I've snowboarded, though, but I'm not very good."

"It takes practice, the best slopes are up near you."

I sit back in my chair and smile at her. "How do you know where I live?"

She smiles and looks away. "It's a small town."

I laugh, and her eyes go to my throat. "Yeah, I guess it is. You hungry?"

"Yes."

"Okay then, stay here while I grab the food."

CHAPTER 7

Cherie

I watch him as he opens cupboards and finds plates, knives, forks, and even napkins. Not once does Eric ask me where anything is. He glances at me and smiles, and I feel it straight to my core. Not in a long time has a man had such an effect on me. The way his shirt tightens across his back as he bends and opens the oven to retrieve the food is enough to get my heart rate up.

It's nice to have a man wait on me for a change. Eric places the food on the plates and brings them to me, then goes back for the cutlery. He stops and rips off some paper towels from the roll, placing it over his arm as he saunters toward me.

"Dinner is served, my lady," exclaims Eric, trying to look and sound like a posh waiter.

Spark

"Thank you. It's weird to have someone feed me in my own home."

He frowns at me, sits down, and cocks his head to the side. "I figured, since your feet were sore, that you'd like someone to take care of you."

I'm speechless. All the boyfriends I've had and not one of them has shown me so much consideration. I smile at him and stuff a huge mouthful of mashed potatoes into my mouth, so I don't have to say anything.

Eric laughs, and his whole face lights up. "Babe? Seriously? How hungry are you? I'm sure your pretty little mouth couldn't take much more."

A blush creeps its way up my face as I have visions of putting something else in my mouth.

"I haven't eaten all day."

"Ahh, that explains it. So, where are we going tomorrow?" asks Eric.

"You still want to go? After what happened at The Roadhouse?"

"Gil is a dick. We should have stayed to prove he didn't get under your skin, but I get it. It's a small town, people talk. It has nothing to do with me wanting to take you to lunch."

I look down at my plate, unsure about what to say next. He's right, I shouldn't have let Gil have the upper hand, but I'm so over the bullshit. The people in this town think they know me since I grew up here, but none of them do. I've changed, and I'm not my family. I'm me, and I'm doing the best I can.

"What if we sneak into The Tarn? I could make a picnic."

"The Tarn?" Eric asks.

"It's only about a ten-minute drive. It's really called Goose Pasture Tarn, but everyone shortens it to The Tarn. It's a privately-owned lake. You're only supposed to go there if you live there. But I know a way in no one knows about. The water is clear, and there's plenty of places to go swimming. The best part about it is there won't be anyone around as it's a workday, so we won't get caught."

Eric raises his eyebrows at me. "Sounds like you're trying to get me into trouble."

"Nah, I've done it loads of times. Trust me."

Eric looks me solemnly in the eyes. "Okay, I'll trust you. But if we get caught, it's every man for himself."

My laughter fills the room, and I nod vigorously at him. "Deal."

"Where's your phone?" asks Eric.

I stand and get it out of my bag. As I hand it to him, I look at him questioningly.

"So, I can ring you tomorrow if I'm running late."

I nod and smile, watching as he quickly enters his number into my phone. His hands are large, grease embedded into the creases and his nails.

Eric grins at me, hands the phone back, and begins cutting into his steak. For a while, we're silent, both enjoying the company and the meal. I stand and walk to my iPod, then Lady Antebellum fills the air.

Eric glances at me and grins. "Country? Should have guessed."

"What's that supposed to mean?"

"You live in a small country town, and you listen to country. Doesn't take a brain surgeon to figure that one out."

There's something in his tone, it's mocking, and I find it slightly offensive so I hit skip. Five Finger Death Punch fills the air.

I watch as Eric chokes on his meal, my taste in music clearly throws him. Smiling, I sit down across from him as he tries to swallow some of his beer to wash it down.

"Thrash music?" splutters Eric.

"This isn't thrash, it's heavy. I do have some thrash if you'd like to listen to it?"

"No, I'm good. You're full of surprises, aren't you?"

"What, I'm not a small-town girl who listens to country? I listen to a lot of different types of music, even classical. But I have to admit I only listen to classical when I'm depressed. Somehow, it seems to lift my spirits to better heights."

Eric is studying me intently so much so, I fidget in my chair, then pick up the beer bottle and play with its label, avoiding his gaze.

"My grandfather used to say, classical music was sent from the gods to soothe our tortured souls." I look at him, and a lazy smile works its way across his face. "Mind you, Da also said a good woman will love you, keep you, protect you, and soothe you if you treat her right."

"So, basically, if you don't have a woman, classical music will do?"

Laughter rumbles up out of his chest as he nods in agreement. I smile at him, enjoying the sound of it as he tries to regain his composure.

"Well, maybe Da didn't have it all quite figured out," replies Eric with his gorgeous smile.

I grin at him and take a swig of my beer. "I don't know, he sounds pretty smart to me. Is he still with us?"

"No, he died a few years back." Eric looks down at his tattoo. "My brothers and I all got this to remember him by. A daily reminder to leave this world better than we found it."

"Brothers?" I ask.

Eric looks away from me, lips pursed, he stands and says, "It's late. I should be going."

I'm confused, I thought we were getting on well, and I was re-thinking my rule of not having sex with him.

I stand slowly. "Did I say something wrong?"

"N-No! I'm tired is all. Long day." He runs a hand through his hair and gives me a half-smile. "See you tomorrow. Twelve sound good?"

"Sure. Yeah, twelve works. See you then."

Eric nods and stalks out the door.

I'm left standing, staring at the space he was in, wondering what I said to make him bolt for the door. I mentally replay the conversation, but I don't think I said anything offensive. Bewildered, I shake my head, lock the front door, leave the dirty dishes on the table, and head for my bed. Eric is right, it has been a long day.

CHAPTER 8

Eric

The trip home is done at break-neck speed as I try and exercise the demons that are pouring out of my soul. I have no business getting involved with this woman. I can't tell her anything too detailed about myself, and I've already said too much talking about my da. I'm putting my family at risk by discussing them with her.

What if she tells someone? The whole fucking reason I'm here is to keep them safe. I need to be smarter about this.

When I reach my front door, I don't remember the trip home. I've done it on auto-pilot, and that can get you killed. All it takes is something to dash out in front of you when you are on a bike, and in a split second, you have to make a decision that could save your life or end it.

Spark

I put the key into the lock of my front door and enter. Nothing is out of place, it's exactly the way I left it earlier—neat, tidy, and lonely.

Am I lonely?

Has it been so long since I've had the company of a woman, I'm willing to take the first one who's shown me any interest? A resounding 'no' fills my head.

This one is different. She's got a fire in her. I'd like to explore this a little further and see where it leads. Cherie has an awesome body, and her smile could light up a room. I need to see if I can get her to do it more than she does.

I throw my keys on the dining table, take off my jacket, and sling it across the back of one of the chairs. Absently, I walk into the kitchen and turn on the coffee maker. There's no use in trying to sleep, so I might as well enjoy a cup or two while I read or listen to music.

Visions of Cherie surface in my mind. She's a beautiful woman, sexy as hell, and complicated. *Or is she a complication for me?* I grab my coffee and take a sip. Flicking on the radio, the late-night news comes on. I sit on my sofa and listen to it. Nothing of interest is on. My mind keeps taking me back to my family and Cherie.

She doesn't know the real me.

She *can't* know the real me.

I'm here to protect my family.

I can't get involved with a woman who could potentially jeopardize everything, even one as sexy and feisty as Cherie. The whole reason I'm here is to protect the ones I love, and I would never want to endanger anyone in my new life. It's selfish of me to begin something on a lie, but visions of her cloud my brain. Maybe it's possible to keep them separate. One of the reasons I haven't gotten close to anyone in this town is I'm not a good liar, and sooner or later someone will catch me out. It's easier to remain alone, but images of her haunt me. My cell phone begins to ring, drawing me out of my inner turmoil.

"Hello?"

"Eric, it's Cherie."

"Hey, is everything okay?" I ask.

"Yeah, about tomorrow? I forgot I had an appointment in town. I'm so sorry, but I'm going to have to cancel."

I should feel relieved. Instead, I'm disappointed.

"Okay, ahh, yeah. Another time?" I ask, hoping she'll say yes even if it's selfish on my part.

"Sure, another time. Thank you for tonight. See you around town." The fake cheerfulness in her voice arouses my curiosity.

"It's a small town, I'm sure you will."

"Night."

She doesn't even wait for me to say goodbye as she clicks off.

This pisses me off. Tomorrow I think I'll pay her a visit. I have the day off anyway, so what harm can it do?

My inner voice tells me it's a bad idea. Cherie's made it easy on me by blowing me off. Maybe it's because she made the decision and not me, but it feels like a challenge, and I haven't had one of those in a while. Everything in this town has become easy and familiar. Cherie seems hard and complicated.

Perhaps I need a distraction?

She's one sexy distraction.

CHAPTER 9

Cherie

It's housework day. I detest it, but it's got to be done some time, right? The dinner from last night is still on the dinner table, all congealed and doesn't look so good the next day. The takeaway containers are placed in the bin. Thankfully, I only need to wash up the cutlery and a couple of plates, which I do fairly quickly. Now, it's time to vacuum, but I only do it with the music up very loud. Searching through my CDs, I'm looking for an album which will help me get everything done quickly. My hand lingers on The Grinders' 'Random Meaning,' and I pop it into the player. It's one of their older titles, and Kat Saunders is singing. Damn, that woman had a wonderful voice.

I put my hair up in a messy bun, start singing along to the music, and dance while vacuuming my floors. Slowly, I make my way through the house, and I'm in the last room—my bedroom—when a hand clamps down on my shoulder. Fear overtakes me, I scream and turn around, hitting the intruder as hard as I can with my vacuum cleaner.

"Ouch! Jesus, Cherie, it's me, Eric."

"What the hell are you doing?" I shriek at him.

"I knocked, I yelled, you didn't answer, and your front door was open, so I let myself in," growls Eric as he rubs the top of his head.

I push past him to the living room and turn off the music. Eric follows me out, wincing as he examines his head.

"I'm so sorry. I reacted. Does it hurt?"

"Only when I breathe." Eric looks me in the eyes, and they seem to sparkle. I can't help it, and I begin to giggle. "It's not funny."

"It kinda is. Sit down. Can I get you anything?" I ask as my laughter takes hold.

Eric grins at me and chuckles. "I didn't realize vacuums could be so dangerous."

It's the end of me, and I clutch my sides as I laugh. It takes me a minute, but I manage to stop laughing.

"Can I get you a coffee?" I ask, grinning like a fool.

"That would be good."

Eric sits down at the dinner table and watches me as I walk into the kitchen. I glance at what I'm wearing—black yoga pants and an oversized white top with the word 'love' written on it. Inwardly, I cringe. I look awful, and my hair must be a mess. I pour two cups of coffee and place one of them in front of him.

"I thought you had an appointment today?" asks Eric as he takes a sip.

Crap. I lied to him last night. Getting involved with him is a bad idea.

"I did, they canceled," I reply quickly.

"Good, means we can still do something today."

"Why are you here if you thought I was out?"

"I came to fix your screen door," answers Eric.

Great. Now, I really feel bad. He came to do something nice, and I hit him over the head with my vacuum, and I lied to him.

"You don't have to do that. It's been like it for a while. It's fine, really…" my words trail off as he quirks an eyebrow at me and cocks his head to the side.

"Cherie, why'd you cancel? And I'd like the truth."

I take a sip of my coffee and look down at the cup. Without meeting his eyes, I say, "You left in such a hurry last night, I thought I'd let you off the hook."

"You thought I *needed* to be let off the hook? So you canceled?"

I meet his gaze and nod.

He purses his lips together and shakes his head. "You got me talking last night about my family. It's not something I like to talk about, and I handled it badly. I'm sorry."

His confession surprises me. The way he talks about his family, you can tell there's a lot of love there. Something very bad must have happened for him not to want to talk about them. I have so many questions I can't ask as I don't want to spook him again.

"Family can be difficult, and you don't have to share if you don't want to. As for today, surely you have something better to do than hang out with me?" I say with fake joviality.

"No friends, remember?"

"Right... I still have a few things to do."

"That's okay. I can fix your door while you do what you need to do," states Eric like
he's decided for us.

"Okay, but I could be a while."

"That's fine. I'll get started on the door." Eric stands with his coffee and walks outside, leaving me sitting at the table wondering what the hell I'm getting myself into.

Leaving my coffee on the table, I walk back into my bedroom to finish vacuuming. Then I strip my bed and put the sheets into the washing machine. Next, I walk into the bathroom. I close the door, strip off, and get into the shower. The hot water feels good. I wash my hair and do what I need to do. The water starts to go cold, and I finally get out of the shower. I wrap a towel around my hair and another around my body. Upon opening the door I find Eric on the other side.

"Eric?"

His gaze starts at my feet and travels up to my towel-clad head. Eric looks me in the eyes and smiles. It's sexy, and I'm very conscious of how little I have on.

"Your door is fixed. Would you like me to hang out your washing?" he asks.

"Y-Yes, thank you," I stammer under his scorching gaze.

Eric does a quick head to toe of me again and walks away. I quickly go into my bedroom and shut the door, letting out the breath I didn't know I was holding. Rummaging through my drawers, I find my nicest black lace bra and panties—a girl needs to be prepared. Opening my closet I find a cute black tee and some denim shorts. I check myself out in the mirror. My hair is a mess, so I drag a comb through it, trying to get it to look at least tidy. The one good thing about this heat is my hair takes no time to dry.

When I walk back out to the dining room, Eric is sitting there, drinking a fresh cup of coffee.

"So, what did you want to do today?" I ask.

"I'd still like to take you to lunch," replies Eric.

"Okay, we could drive to Frisco, it's only half an hour away. Vinny's Restaurant has great food."

"Sounds good." Eric stands and walks toward me. "Now, the only question is..." he licks his lips and drops his gaze to my mouth, "... are we going to go on my bike or in your car? Personally, I think my bike is safer than your death trap."

I narrow my eyes, flick out a hip, and place a hand on it. "Really? I'll have you know my car is *perfectly* safe." I want so badly to ride on the back of his bike, but now he's dissed my car, how can I?

Eric holds up his hands in surrender and says, "I'm not sure about perfectly safe, but it's a gorgeous day, too good to be stuck inside a car. I brought an extra helmet, please say the bike," Eric says sincerely.

I nod. "Okay, let me get my purse and plait my hair, then we can go."

"Babe, put some jeans on, and do you own a leather jacket?"

"Bossy," I state as I walk back to my bedroom.

In response, I get a deep chuckle, which rocks me to my core.

Chapter 10

Eric

I'm sitting on my bike waiting for Cherie to come out. I'm thinking about how easy it was to convince her to come. There's always a little bit of fight, but she caves fairly quickly and does what I want. Well, most of the time.

The front door opens, and my mouth falls open. Cherie's hair is pulled back in a plait, she has on leather pants and a long leather coat. With her sunglasses on, she looks like a character out of the Matrix but so much hotter.

"What are you wearing?" I ask as I appraise her from head to toe.

"You told me to put on a leather jacket. This is my nicest one. Don't you like it?" Cherie has her hands, palms out, and does a little twirl.

My dick twitches, and I nod frantically at her. "Babe, I more than like it. You look damn fine!"

Cherie stops moving, tilts her head to the side, and chews on her bottom lip. "Really?"

"Come on, you know you look good."

She walks toward me, climbs on, and whispers, "Thank you."

I twist in my seat to lock eyes with her. Unfortunately, with her sunglasses on, I can't read her eyes. I pass her a helmet. "Need to keep you safe, so put this on."

Cherie takes it, gives me a small smile, and puts it on. When it's securely fastened on her head, I grab her hands and wrap them around my waist.

"I'm not going to break any laws, but hold on tight."

I turn my bike on, give it some gas, and off we go. Instinctively, she grips on harder, and we head for Frisco. Cherie directs me with a series of hand gestures, and we arrive at Vinnie's in twenty minutes.

When she gets off the bike, she pulls off her helmet and throws her arms around me. "*That* was fantastic! I had no idea bikes could be this much fun. I'm so sorry I headbutted you a couple of times, but once I got the hang of it and relaxed, it was great."

Her enthusiasm is infectious. I grin, climb off, grab her hand, and walk toward Vinnie's. "We should do a ride along a coastal road. Take off for a week and stay in places along the way. It's a nice way to see the country."

"Yeah, when I win the lottery, we'll do it," replies Cherie with a cheeky grin.

"You know, it's not that expensive. My treat."

She stops walking and pulls on my arm causing me to spin around and face her. "Number one, don't say things you don't mean. Number two, I don't need you to pay for me. I can look after myself." Her eyes are hidden from me by her sunglasses, but from her stance, I can tell she's trying to tell me something important.

Reaching up, I take her glasses off her face, wrap an arm around her waist, and pull her into me. She looks like a startled rabbit, and when my lips first touch hers, she freezes. My other hand wraps around the back of her neck, and slowly I feel her melt into me. Never before has a woman fit me so perfectly. A moan escapes her, and as it does, my tongue slips into her mouth. Her hands go up under my tee, and the kiss gets deeper and more intense. A growl escapes me, and I want to do so much more than kiss her. Cherie's lips are soft, and she tastes amazing. The softness of her body pressed up against the hardness of mine feels good—it feels right.

A wolf whistle pierces the air, followed by, "Get a room."

I stop and look over my shoulder to see a guy getting into a pick-up, shaking his head with a grin on his face. I nod at him and look back at Cherie. Her face is flushed, lips are swollen, and her eyes are filled with lust.

"You keep looking at me like that and, baby, I'll be finding us a room here in town," I whisper.

She shakes her head slightly, moves her hands to my shoulders, takes a deep breath, and pushes me back. "I keep telling you, I can pay for myself."

I chuckle at her and hold out my hand. "Let's go eat."

Cherie smiles, grasps my hand, and leads me into Vinnie's. Once inside, Cherie sits at a table for two. The inside of this place is not like anything I've seen before—dark red ceiling with gold swirls on it, and the walls are painted a mustard color with wood paneling below it.

"This is the pub part of Vinnie's. They make everything here themselves. There's a proper dining room through there." Cherie points behind me. "And the staff here are super nice."

"That's good, babe, but what's the food like?" I ask.

"Our food is the best in the district," gushes a waitress as she places a menu in my hands. "I'm Julie, and I'll be your server today. Now, how hungry are you folks?"

"Starving," I say, grinning at Cherie, who goes a lovely shade of red.

"Good! May I suggest the baby spinach, gorgonzola, crispy bacon, and pickled red onions to start, followed by braised Aspen Ridge short ribs with cream corn sauce and truffle polenta? It's so good."

"Sounds good for me, and a bottle of Shiner Bock for both of us," I say as I nod at Julie.

"And for you, ma'am? What would you like?"

"I'll have the salad you recommended, but could I please have the bolognese ragu?"

"Excellent choice. I'll be back in a jiffy with your drinks." Julie smiles big at us, removes the menus, and bustles away.

Reaching over, I grab Cherie's hand and link my fingers through hers across the table.

"You come here often?"

Cherie shakes her head. "No, I tend to stay in Breckenridge." Her eyes drop to our linked hands, and she frowns slightly. I rub the side of her hand with my thumb, and she looks back at me. "What are we doing?"

"Having lunch?" I grin at her and quirk an eyebrow.

"What did we do outside?"

"You seemed to like it... but if I'm wrong..." I let the words hang in the air.

Cherie disentangles her hand from mine and sits back. "I have lousy taste in men. Epically bad. If there were a picture of someone who can't pick a winner to save herself, it would be me, with flashing lights around it. Tell me you're a good guy, tell me you're not a jerk, tell me I can trust you."

Cherie's eyes are pleading, and I want to be that guy for her, but I can't give her all of me. It's too dangerous for her, my family, and me. I look down at the table. I'm nodding, trying to think of the right words to say. I like this woman. I want to explore this and see where it goes, but I can't tell her everything.

"I can't promise you a lifetime. I can promise I'll treat you right. I don't cheat. I mean what I say, and I say what I mean. I don't have hidden agendas." I look up and lock eyes with her. "I like you. I want to see where this takes us, but it's not all on me. You need to be all those things for me as well." Part of me feels guilty for not telling her everything, but it's early days. This is our second date. I'm not about to pledge feelings of unending love or share with her my most intimate thoughts and truths.

Cherie smiles and nods. "Sorry. I didn't mean for it to turn into an episode of truth or dare."

Julie, our waitress, returns and places a beer in front of each of us. "Starters will be right up."

"Tell me about you." Cherie picks up a beer and puts it to her lips. She puts the bottle down, staring at me intently, waiting for my response. I have the back story the Marshals gave me, and I know it off by heart.

"I grew up on the East Coast, both my parents are dead. Ahh, I thought Breckenridge would be a good place to start over." Even to my ears, it sounds flat and unbelievable.

"That's it?" Cherie asks questioningly.

"I came here to start again, to forget my old life. Not that there was anything wrong with it, but I needed more," I reply with a smile.

"You've lived here for three years, and you've never socialized with anyone except some of the guys from work, and you did it all because you needed more?"

"I'm boring. I don't make friends easily. I like working with my hands. I used to do clerical work back East, but I've always had a love for anything mechanical. I'm good with machinery." The lies, mixed with truth, slip out of my mouth easily, but I can tell she's not buying it.

Cherie has her head tilted to the side, processing what I've said. She opens her mouth to ask me something when the waitress returns and puts our salads in front of us.

"Enjoy," exclaims Julie as she walks away.

"I'm starved. Let's eat."

Cherie studies me for a few seconds more as I pretend to be engrossed in my meal. Eventually,

Spark

she picks up a fork and begins to eat. The silence between us is so thick you could cut it with a knife. I'm trying to make it feel like I'm not bothered, but the longer the silence stretches on, the harder it is for me to engage her in conversation.

"How's your salad?" asks Cherie.

I've been eating it without tasting it. Putting my fork down, I look into her eyes. "It's good. How's yours?"

"Everything's better with bacon." A small smile plays on her lips, and I can feel the tension drop a notch.

"Woman after my own heart. So, what do you want to do after lunch?" My mind immediately goes to finishing what we started outside, and my dick twitches.

"I was thinking we could visit my granddaddy, if it's okay?"

"It wasn't what I was thinking, but yeah, sounds good. I need to give him an update on the 'stang."

"What were you thinking?" Cherie asks innocently.

A chuckle escapes me. "I bet you'd look great naked in my bed."

Her face and neck turn a pretty shade of pink, and she looks down at her plate. "Y-You live on the side of a mountain, right?" stutters Cherie.

"Yeah, babe. It's not much, but it's enough."

Her head snaps up, and she scrutinizes me. "See, that's what I don't get about you. You came here to start over and change, but Eric, you seem to be living on the edge of society, not embracing a new life but hiding from it."

Fuck.

She's summed me up perfectly.

"It takes me a while to warm up to people, that's all. When was the last time you visited your grandfather?" I ask to change the subject.

Cherie frowns and replies, "A few days ago."

The rest of our starter is eaten in silence. Julie comes back to us in a fluster.

"Did you enjoy your meal?" asks Julie as she takes our plates away. "The rest won't be far away."

Grateful to have something to hang on to, I pick up the beer and take a swig. I look at Cherie, and she's staring out the window. This isn't how I wanted today to go. I stand and move my chair from across the table so I'm sitting to her left, then take her hand in mine. "I like you. I'm being as honest with you as I can. I'm not a dick. Although, I do have one," I say, trying to be funny.

Cherie quirks an eyebrow at me and smiles. "Good to know."

I raise her hand to my lips and brush her knuckles with a kiss. A sigh escapes her. "You sure you don't want to come back to my place?"

Cherie hesitates but answers firmly. "Yes, I'm sure."

The look on her face doesn't match her answer, so I turn her wrist over and kiss it. "Positive?"

"You don't fight fair, Eric."

"Are we fighting?"

"No and yes. I feel like you're keeping things from me, and I don't know why."

I link my fingers with hers and nod. "Doesn't hurt to keep a little bit of mystery, does it?"

Smiling, she answers, "So long as you don't turn into a lying son of a bitch. No."

"Fair enough," I answer with a chuckle.

The rest of the meal is spent in pleasant conversation. Nothing too deep on my part. Cherie doesn't ask me anything about my past life. I can't help but think she's going easy on me.

CHAPTER 11

Cherie

I'm playing the part. Eric clearly doesn't want me to get too close to him. I've been hurt too many times to let him into my life without him sharing *something* about himself. Maybe he's divorced. Maybe he's got a bunch of kids out there he doesn't want me to know about. Who knows?

The attraction between us is strong, but I will *not* allow myself to fall so easily for a nice smile and a good body. Been there, done that, not doing it again. He'll make a nice friend, no acquaintance. It's not good to allow myself to be around someone I find attractive and not sleep with them. Let's face it, if he kisses me again as he did outside, all my resolve will be gone.

Dammit! Eric seems like such a good guy.

"Earth to Cherie. Babe… you in there?"

Spark

"Sorry, thinking about my granddaddy. Are you done? I'd like to see him." I smile up at him brightly, and he smiles back. This alone is enough to make me melt.

"Sure, babe, I'll go pay. Meet you outside." We stand, and Eric kisses my cheek. I give him another smile, nod, and walk outside.

This is not going to be easy. I sigh and stretch, trying to ease the tension I'm feeling and reminding myself I deserve to be treated well. *Fuck that*, like a queen.

Arms wrap around my waist, and I feel Eric's hot breath near my ear. "Damn, woman, you look good."

My thighs light up, but my head kicks in. I reach down and grab his hands, twisting myself out of his embrace. "Well, thank you," I say with a little too much enthusiasm. Eric frowns and looks at me with a confused look on his face. "Let's get this baby on the road." I lightly punch his arm and gesture toward the bike.

"Is everything okay?"

"Yes! I'm eager to see my granddaddy."

Eric climbs on the bike, and I hop on behind him. I have no choice but to hold onto him.

"You good?" Eric asks.

"Yeah, I'm good."

I pay no attention to where we are going until we hit a gravel drive and are heading up a driveway.

Dammit. He's taken me to his home.

I climb off and stumble as I rip the helmet from my head.

"What the fuck?" I ask.

Eric climbs off and smiles. "I needed to get something from inside and didn't think you'd mind seeing where I live?"

My inner voice is screaming at me for being so stupid. I should have driven. I frown at him. "I'm surprised, that's all." Turning around, I look at the view. It's gorgeous. I feel Eric standing beside me, both of us absorbed in our own thoughts. I chance a glimpse at him to find him staring down at me. "It's a lovely view."

"Yeah, it is," replies Eric. His fingers lightly touch the side of my face before he turns and goes inside his home.

I follow him inside. It's not very big and very manly in the decoration. Eric is over near the bed going through a drawer.

"Find what you're looking for?" He nods but doesn't turn around. "Mind if I help myself to some water?"

Spark

"It's fine, glasses in the cupboard above the sink to the left."

I move into the kitchen and grab a glass. Opening the fridge, I search for cold water.

"Eric—" I shout as I turn around, and he's right there. "Jesus! You scared me."

"Sorry. What are you looking for?"

"Cold water." He's standing too close, and I feel trapped between him and the fridge.

Eric smiles and shakes his head. "I don't like water in the fridge, so there is none. The faucet works."

"We're having a heatwave, and you don't have water in the fridge?"

"Yeah, but in the future, for you, I'll make sure I have some." Eric winks at me and moves to sit at the kitchen table.

I fill my glass from the tap and sit beside him. "Did you find what you were looking for?" I ask.

"Truthfully, I wanted to show you where and how I live. It's not much, but it's comfortable." He's avoiding my eyes and looks a little sheepish.

I'm not sure what to say, so in true Cherie style, I go with humor. "Ahh, so this is a kidnapping? Gotta tell you, buddy, you won't want to keep me, after all. I like *cold* water." I laugh at myself, and Eric locks eyes with me, not laughing.

"I think I could get used to cold water."

My laughter dies. Slowly, he reaches up and places a hand at the back of my head pulling me closer to him. As his lips are about to connect with mine, I shake my head.

"You have too many secrets," I whisper.

"I promise, I don't," he whispers back.

Eric closes the gap, and my mouth opens letting his tongue duel with mine. My body has a will of its own, and I rise and straddle him on the chair. He groans with pleasure as I grind into him. Eric's hands are everywhere. They travel my body, but when he massages my breast, I know I'm lost.

Eric's hands go to my ass, and he stands, taking me with him. The next thing I know he's laying me down gently on the bed.

"You know you're too much trouble," whispers Eric as he kisses my neck. "Knew it from the moment I laid eyes on you, and I've thought of nothing but you since."

I grip his face in my hands, forcing him to look me in the eyes. "And you have too many secrets. If you lie to me, I'll cut your balls off."

Eric grins. "Fair trade."

His mouth closes over mine, silencing us both. Eric pulls up my T-shirt, his hands touching the lacy bra underneath. I arch into him, and he growls. I open my legs, and he places his knee between them. Grinding into his knee, I groan in frustration at the amount of clothing separating us.

"Stop!" Immediately Eric is off me and standing beside the bed, his breath is ragged. "Take a step back." Confusion crosses his features, but he does as he's told. "Now, take off your clothes." The confusion fades into passion as he smirks at me and slowly peels off what he's wearing. I stand and remove my coat, letting it fall onto his floorboards, then I sit down and remove my boots. When I look up, Eric is naked. He's over six feet of muscle. No more tattoos, a toned body and a very large, erect cock.

I stand, take two steps, and grip his cock in my hand, pumping it.

"No," growls Eric. "Take off your clothes."

The T-shirt comes off in one fluid movement, but the leather pants are another matter. I undo the button and zipper and slowly peel them over my ass, but there's no way I'm getting these off in a sexy manner.

"Sit down," orders Eric. "Allow me."

I fall onto the bed, leather pants at my knees.

Eric reaches out and pulls me to him, burying his face at my core. I feel his tongue flick out and lick at me through my underwear. Gripping his head to me, I groan as he continues his assault. All I can think of is, *this would be much better if I were naked*. As if he can read my thoughts, Eric pulls my underwear and then upon reaching my leather pants at my knees he pulls them down and off in one fluid movement. Smiling, I crawl up the bed, legs spread, waiting for him.

The look in his eyes is predatory as he advances on me. This is no gentle lover. He goes straight to my clit and sucks. His eyes never leave mine as his mouth teases, sucks, and licks at my core. I spread my legs further and hold onto his head, grinding into him. My whole body is on fire, and as I'm about to shatter, Eric stops. His mouth smothers my groan of frustration, and his tongue teases mine. I can feel his cock pressed against my stomach, so I reach for it, and Eric growls into me.

"I need you."

"Soon," he whispers.

My body has other ideas. I move further up the bed, grab his cock, and position it at my entrance. He enters me, then pulls out. In frustration, I arch up, taking all of him. Not to be outdone, Eric pulls out and moves back down the bed.

"I. Need. You," I say loudly.

Eric chuckles. "I'm not done pleasing you yet. I want you satisfied. It's been a long time, and I'm not going to last long." His tone of voice is commanding, and I do as I'm told.

Frustrated, I close my eyes and fall back, only to open them in surprise as Eric's tongue delves into my folds, bringing with it a burning electric feeling which consumes my body, and I climax screaming his name.

Spark

Slowly, I come down, my hands moving to his shoulders. "Tell me what you want me to do," I whisper.

My body is liquid fire, and at this moment, I will do anything he asks.

"I'm going to fuck you. I'm going to make you mine."

I smile lazily at him. "Honey, after that, you can do whatever you want."

The grin I receive in return is sexy as sin. Eric kisses his way up my body, caressing, loving, stroking every inch of me. When he gets to my mouth, he takes possession of it. Then, in one swift motion, he enters me. My body expands, making room for this wanted assault. Slowly, Eric moves in and out. His eyes never leave mine, and his jaw is clenched as though he's trying not to lose control.

"Eric, let go," I whisper. He shakes his head. "Baby, it's all good."

I begin to move in unison with him, focusing on his cock moving in and out of me, clenching myself around him with every thrust.

"Fuck, Cherie, you keep doing that, and honey… I'm not going to last."

Eric rises off me, his hands planted on either side of me as he increases his speed. I match him thrust for thrust and can feel my body searching for another release.

"Wait for me," I plead.

Eric's face twists in frustration. "Not sure I can. You did tell me to let go."

"Baby, I'm nearly there."

Reaching down, I work myself, and Eric smiles. "Fuck, you're beautiful," he growls.

That's all it takes to push me over the edge. My pussy contracts, Eric yells, pumps into me twice more, and then collapses on top of me.

Rising, Eric looks down at me, his eyes filled with lust and possession. He kisses both nipples, my mouth, and then rolls off. I groan at the loss of him, but he places an arm under my head and a leg over me, pulling me in closer.

Neither of us say anything, and within a matter of minutes, I'm asleep, safely wrapped up in this man.

CHAPTER 12

Eric

Cherie falls asleep almost instantly but not me. I'm plagued with guilt over what I've done. When she screamed 'Eric,' I nearly stopped. Well, I *thought* about it.

Extracting myself from her sleeping form without waking her isn't easy, but I manage it. Quietly, I go into the bathroom and close the door. I stare at my reflection and want to punch the mirror. Cherie specifically asked me *not to be a jerk*, and I'm starting this relationship off with lies.

Relationship? Fuck!

Yet, I know it's true.

There's no way I'm letting her get away.

I turn on the cold water in the shower and step under its hard spray. I stay in until my fingers prune, and the whole time I'm trying to figure out a way to let Cherie know the truth, but it all keeps coming back to Heather and how I got her killed. I won't let it happen again. I'm *not* putting her in danger. This time I know who all the players are. If I keep her separate, Cherie will be safe.

At last, I turn off the water and get out, towel myself off and go into the kitchen. I fill up the coffee maker, wait until it's brewed, then pour myself a cup. I turn around a dining chair, so I can watch Cherie's sleeping form. The hospital's visiting hours are from ten in the morning until eight o'clock at night, so I let her sleep. It doesn't get dark this time of year until eight thirty at night, so we have plenty of time.

I'm on my second cup of coffee, still sitting in my towel when Cherie sits up. The sheet I'd draped over her falls to her waist exposing her breasts. She stretches languorously and yawns, her back arches, and she sort of shakes herself. It takes her a full minute to realize she's not in familiar surroundings. Cherie's hands grab the sheet pulling it up, and eventually, her eyes find mine.

"Hey, beautiful, how you feeling?"

"I broke a promise to myself."

I chuckle. "Is that so?"

"Yeah, I told myself I wasn't going to sleep with you."

"If it makes you feel any better, I didn't sleep," I tease.

Spark

Cherie frowns at me. "What time is it?"

"It's a little after six. Do you want to go visit your grandfather?" She nods and swings her legs off the bed with the sheet clutched to her front. "Honey, is something wrong?"

"I need my clothes."

I stand and pick them up off the floor, putting them beside her on the bed. "Anything else?"

Cherie smiles and looks down at the floor, face flushed. "I need a towel."

"They are in the bathroom." I point to the bathroom door, and she shakes her head slightly. "Honey, don't tell me you're embarrassed? I've kissed every inch of you. There's nothing left to see."

With her lips pressed together and her blush deepening, she looks up at me. "I know that but…" Her eyes fall to the floor.

"Look at me, Cherie."

When her eyes reach mine, I take off my towel and hand it to her. Cherie looks slightly embarrassed and a little amused as she stares at my cock.

"You have nothing to be ashamed of. I like you, you like me, and we have plenty of time to work this out."

Cherie nods, puts the towel to her front, and walks into the bathroom, exposing her back half for me to see. "Like the view?" she asks, mischievously.

"You have a nice ass."

Cherie turns, winks, and continues to walk backward, grinning at me. "You know, Eric, so do you." When she hits the bathroom, she closes the door.

I shake my head. *Women*. I don't think I'll ever fully understand them.

CHAPTER 13

Cherie

What have I done?

I had sex with Eric, *that's what I've done!*

The man is so confusing, and yet I've never had a man treat me with such care, such devotion, and doing it all in a possessive, bossy manner. I like it, maybe a little too much. Eric is so eager to please me. I know he's keeping secrets, but I believe him when he says he likes me. I believe him when he says he's not a jerk, but my inner voice keeps berating me. And when he says he wanted to make me his, my body responded with a joyous *yes*. It seems my body wants this man even if my head is trying to point out he's not being completely truthful. Hopefully, in time, he'll share everything with me.

The trip to the hospital takes about forty minutes, and this time, I don't headbutt him at all. The exhilaration I feel being on the back of the bike, Eric's bike, is better than anything, well, except sex.

Eric pulls up in the parking lot of the hospital, and I quickly jump off. He climbs off, grabs my hand, and we walk into the hospital. A small smile plays on his lips as he links his finger through mine.

"You're amazing, you know that?" asks Eric.

"You're not so bad yourself." I go up on my tiptoes and lightly brush his lips with mine. I wink at him and tug him toward the elevators.

We are walking across the lobby when a man approaches us. He stops about two feet away, eyes locked with Eric. He's well-dressed in a black suit, slicked-back blond hair, and a scar down his left cheek.

"It's good to see you, Maddock."

Eric stops and pulls me back. "I'm sorry, I think you have me confused with someone else," replies Eric and attempts to go around him.

"Yeah, see, I don't think so. You going to introduce me to your friend, Maddock?"

The man's eyes flick to me, and I can tell by Eric's stance he doesn't want me anywhere near him.

"Look, mister, you've got the wrong guy. My name is Eric Hill."

"Nah, it's Maddock MacKenny. We both know it. Now, we can do this the easy way, and no one gets

Spark

hurt, or we can do this the hard way." The man smiles and looks me up and down. "I think I'm going to like doing it the hard way."

Eric purses his lips together and looks at me. "Babe, go visit your granddaddy, and I'll be up in a minute."

"Is everything okay, Eric?" I ask.

"Now, sugar, everything is fine," replies the man.

I glance at the man, then look at Eric. He smiles and nods. "Yeah, babe, it's a case of wrong identity. You go ahead while I talk to this nice man here. Sort him out."

I let go of Eric's hand and give the man a wide berth. He tracks me until I am well away. I stop at the elevators and look back at them. Eric has moved and is standing chest to chest with the man. He doesn't look happy, and from the way their conversation is going, I can tell they are about to come to blows. The elevator doors open, but I don't enter. I head back toward Eric when a hand clamps down on my arm.

"Don't say a word. Come with me." I feel something jab into my side, and I look down to see a gun. I look back up, my assailant is a large black man who smiles at me as he pulls me toward the doors of the hospital.

I look for Eric, he's staring at me, he nods and mouths, *'It's okay.'*

This is not okay.

Is he fucking Eric or Maddock?

And who the hell is walking me out of this hospital?

I know if this guy gets me to where he's going, I'm as good as dead, so I say, "I don't feel so good. It's why we're at the hospital."

"Sugar, we're going for a car ride, then a plane. You'll do as you're told."

I let my body go slack, and hit the floor inside the hospital doors. A nurse comes running to my side. The black guy looks down and swears.

"Ma'am, are you okay?" asks the nurse.

"The baby. It must be the baby," I shriek.

The man who was trying to get me out of the hospital backs away from me and disappears through the doors. I look back to where Eric was, but he's gone.

The nurse yells, "We need a chair. Now!"

An orderly runs over, they help me into it and rush me to the emergency department.

I grab the nurse's arm. "I need security, and I need them now."

"Let's get you onto the bed, then we'll get security. Okay?"

"No, you don't understand. The man who was with me had a gun, he was trying to take me," I shriek at her.

She immediately turns, walks out of my cubicle, and returns with a security guard.

Spark

"Ma'am, is there a problem?"

"There was a man, he had a gun, and he was trying to get me to leave the hospital with him. You need to do something."

He takes a couple of steps back and motions for another guard to join us.

"Pete, can you wait here with the lady while I call the police?"

He nods, and I begin to pace.

Eric has gone, he's obviously in trouble.

"Ma'am, you need to calm down," says Pete in a soothing tone.

"What I need to do is figure out what the fucking hell is going on!"

CHAPTER 14

Eric

They got me into a car as Cherie hit the floor inside the hospital. At first, I thought he'd done something to her, but when he got into the car, he explodes.

"Fucking bitch caused a scene. They'll be looking at camera footage now, and our faces are going to be everywhere."

I laugh, and the black guy punches me in the face.

"Shut. The. Fuck. Up!" he roars.

The man who escorted me into the car laughs. "Rio, my man, calm down. So what? We aren't wanted anywhere. Well, not here in the states, anyway. Be cool. We got who we came for."

"Yeah, we did. Maddock MacKenny, we've been looking for you for a long, long, time. I was starting to think you really were dead."

"Fellas, you have me confused with someone else. My name is Eric Hill," I say as I rub my jaw.

Rio pulls out a knife and holds it to my wrist, then he twists it, slicing through my jacket.

"Nah, see this here?" he asks, pointing to my tattoo. "This is how we know it's you, all you MacKenny boys have one."

Fuck.

"A lot of people have this tattoo."

Rio laughs, and so does his scarred friend. "Yeah, sure they do."

"Doesn't matter anyway. We're taking you home. Someone wants to see you in person, your old boss, and if you aren't Maddock, we'll kill you anyway," says the scarred one.

I glare at both of them.

I'm fucked.

I need to buy some time.

"And how are you getting me back to Washington?"

"Funny, if you're not Maddock, how do you know where you're from?"

"Look, Scarface, I'm dead either way. So, why pretend?" I growl out.

"Scarface? Is that the best you got? I'm going to enjoy skinning you alive. My name is Louis, and we're flying you back."

I still have time.

A plane.

It must be private.

They won't risk taking me through an airport.

My hands are bound with zip ties at my front, but my feet aren't.

CHAPTER 15

Cherie

The police came and took me to the station. They showed me footage of the man who tried to take me. I told them about the conversation with the first man and how he called Eric, Maddock MacKenny. I've been sitting in an interrogation room by myself for over an hour, but it's more than six hours since Eric was taken. The door is open, and people look in on me from time to time, and finally, the sheriff comes in, closes the door, and sits down.

"We did some digging. It appears Eric Hill is an alias for Maddock MacKenny." He searches my face looking for something. "You didn't know, did you?"

"No, Sheriff, I didn't. I don't know him that well. We've been out a couple of times. He's been working at the garage. Do they know anything?"

Heat infuses my face as I think about Eric and me in bed.

"Call me, Frank. We've spoken to the owner of the garage, and he doesn't know anything. All we've managed to find is this." He opens a folder and flips over a photograph of Eric. He's in a suit, smiling, looking happy, standing next to a group of men. "This is Maddock MacKenny, does he look like Eric?"

"Yes, it's him. A little younger but—"

"Maddock MacKenny is dead. Well, that's what the feds tell us, which is weird they'd even know."

"What does that mean?"

"It means he's in witness protection. Well, that's what we think it means." Frank runs a hand over his face and looks at me. "Maddock was killed along with his sister in a car bombing three years ago. If this is him, it's the only explanation."

"Have you talked to the feds?" I ask.

"We have. So far, we're getting nowhere. The car Eric... Maddock... whoever the hell he is, got into didn't have plates. We're running the faces of those two men through facial recognition, but it takes time. You should go home, Miss Lake. We'll let you know if we find anything. I can have one of my officers drop you off."

I stand. "Thank you, Sheriff... I mean Frank. I appreciate it."

Spark

Frank escorts me out the front to a waiting deputy, and he drives me home. I live only a little out of town, so it doesn't take long. When we pull up, I climb out of the cruiser, and the deputy waits until I've unlocked my front door and opened it, then he drives away.

I close the door and lean against it, grateful to be home and surrounded by my things. I take two steps inside the door when I realize I'm not alone. Turning, I open the door, but someone slams it shut.

"Be calm. We aren't here to hurt you. All we want to know is… is Maddock alive?"

My heart feels like it's in my throat. Someone turns on a light, and I'm staring at a hand with long fingers and he's holding the door shut. I close my eyes, scared. If I don't see their faces, they might let me go.

"I don't know who that is," I whisper.

"Right, you know him as Eric. It's Cherie, right? Cherie, I'm going to show you something, so I need you to open your eyes."

I shake my head. "No, I haven't seen your faces. You can leave, I won't tell anyone."

"I told you sitting in the dark like this was going to scare her, didn't I? Jesus, fucking Christ, Angus!"

"And I told *you* the cops aren't going to help us get Maddock back. No one is."

"Who the fuck is Maddock?" I yell as I turn around, causing both of them to stare at me, and I realize I'm staring at them. "*Fuck.*"

The man, Angus, who's standing closest to me, takes two steps back and holds up his hands.

"I'm Angus MacKenny, and this ugly fucker is my brother, Sean. We've been searching for Maddock and our sister, Heather, for three years."

Angus is dressed in black and is a little thin. He has a beanie on his head and is wearing thick, black-rimmed glasses. Sean is in jeans, a cut, and a black T-shirt. He has one of those chains that goes from his belt loop to his pocket, and I'm assuming a wallet is attached at the other end.

Sean stands and holds out his hand. "Maddock has great taste in women, always did."

Slowly, I place my hand in his. The grip is firm but not bone-crunching. As I stare into his eyes, I can see Eric in there. He has the same look to him only he's a little rougher looking.

"I'm Cherie Lake. Why would your brother be hiding out here under a false name? And who's Heather? And show me your forearm."

"Heather is our sister. We're hoping she's with Maddock. The closest I can tell is, Mad went into witness protection. Over the years, I've found traces of him here and there but nothing on her. It's possible she died in the explosion, but I know Mad is still alive. I *know* it," replies Angus with emphasis as he pulls up his sleeve revealing the same tattoo as Eric. I look at Sean, who simply turns his arm over, and there buried within a sleeve is the cross.

I slowly release a breath and walk around them into the kitchen. Pulling the fridge door open, I grab a bottle of beer, pop the top off, and take a swig.

"Let me get this straight... Eric is Maddock, and you think he's been in witness protection?" I begin to pace in the kitchen. Talking to myself, I say, "Well, that makes sense. All that crap about starting over and wanting a clean slate. Jesus! I'm such an idiot."

"I like her, she's got balls," says Sean as he grins at Angus.

"Where would they have taken him?" I ask.

Angus shrugs. "I'm not sure. We thought you might be able to help us with that."

Sean walks toward me and gestures at the bottle. "You got another one of those?"

Opening the fridge, I pull one out and hand it to him. He twists off the top and tosses it in the sink.

"Did they say anything to you?" asks Sean.

"Yeah, the guy said I was going for a car ride, then a plane."

Both men exchange glances.

"Gotta be the private strip outside of town," says Angus.

"Yeah, man, but it was hours ago. They'd be long gone by now." Sean pulls out his phone. "You think they'd be stupid enough to take him back to DC?"

"Maybe." Angus looks over at me. "Can we hang here until we know where we're going?"

"Sure you—"

"*Fuck that.* I can't sit around here and wait. I need to know," interrupts Sean with frustration in his tone.

"Until we know where he is, it's stupid to go off galavanting around. Cool your jets. Sit. Let me see what planes flew in and out of the strip."

"What if they didn't log a flight plan?" asks Sean.

"Jesus, man, let me look first, okay?" replies Angus as he sits down in front of a laptop and starts clicking away.

"I know someone who works out at the strip. I could make a call?"

Sean looks at me and nods. "Do it."

Taking my phone out of my pocket, I scroll through my contacts until I find the one I'm looking for.

"This is Dylan."

"Hey, Dylan, it's Cherie."

"Yeah, babe, I know, got your number in my phone. What's up?"

"Dylan, have any planes left the strip in the last eight hours?"

"Duh! Yeah, of course."

"I mean, any private planes?"

"Yes, come on, Cherie. What're you looking for?"

"A white guy with a scar and a big black guy."

"Oh, yeah, they had the sweet little Cessna Citation CJ4. It was last year's model. Very nice…" Dylan pauses. "Do you know those guys?"

"Actually, they ripped me off at the diner, didn't pay their bill. Don't suppose you know what time they left and where they were going?"

"Fuckers! Sure do, Cherie. People like that suck. They left here a little over seven hours ago and were headed for…" I can hear him flipping through papers, "… Ronald Reagan Washington National Airport."

"Thank you, Dylan, thank you. Next piece of pie is on me."

Before he can say anything else, I hang up.

"Well?" asks Sean impatiently.

"They're headed for Washington, Ronald Reagan Airport."

Sean looks at Angus. "Let's ride." Both men stand and head for the door.

"Wait! I'm coming with you."

"Like fuck you are," says Sean.

"You don't know what the men look like. I can help."

A look passes between the two men.

Angus shrugs and nods.

"Fine, you got wheels?" asks Sean.

"Yeah, I've got my truck."

Angus laughs. "The piece of crap out front? It'll never keep up. She can ride with you."

"Why can't she ride with you?"

"Boys… let's get going, yeah?" I slip my bag across my body and walk out my front door.

Sean walks out first, and Angus follows, pulling the door shut behind him. I stick close to Sean as he makes his way around to the back of my home where two bikes are parked.

Sean climbs on. "Hop on, princess. We need to get on the road."

As soon as I'm on, he starts his ride. Angus is sitting astride his but doesn't start it.

"You coming?" asks Sean.

"I need to contact Kyle. He's closest."

Sean nods and takes off.

I have no idea what the hell I'm doing. I'm on the back of a bike with a man I don't know, heading to God knows where, in search of a man I don't really know.

And for the first time in my life, I feel like I'm heading in the right direction.

CHAPTER 16

Maddock

I have a hood over my head, and I'm tied to a chair. For the last hour or is it two, I've been trying to loosen the ropes but to no avail. I can hear traffic in the distance and voices in another room. They knocked me out before the plane landed, so I have no idea how long I've been sitting here.

"Good afternoon, Maddock. How are you?"

The hood is removed, and light floods in, blinding me. I blink several times before I can focus on the man in front of me—my old boss, Colin Lamond.

"I'm fine, thank you, Colin, and you?" I reply with sarcasm.

"Oh, you know, hiring mercenaries to find you, spending a small fortune… but hey, they *finally* delivered."

"You're a fucking piece of shit. You know that, Colin?"

"Is that the best you can do?" Colin laughs. "If you'd only died like you were supposed to, this wouldn't even have been necessary."

"Sorry to disappoint you."

"If only you hadn't stuck your nose in where it didn't belong," sneers Colin.

"And if only you hadn't been a scum-sucking pig and *killed* my sister, but we all have our crosses to bear."

Colin laughs and points at me as he walks back and forth in front of me. "Ah, your sweet sister, Heather, right? That's on *you*."

"I came to you because I thought someone was doing the wrong thing. Instead, you betrayed me. How could you use Zed like that? How could you send those fucking terrorists those components? Do you have any idea what they could do in the wrong hands?" I yell at him.

Colin laughs harder, crosses his arms over his chest, and glares down at me. "You made a good accountant, but a lousy snitch. Where do you think all the extra money came from? How do you think we were able to build all those experimental prototypes? All that takes money, so, yes, I sell the odd component to whomever I need to, to keep Zed Fluid Systems afloat."

Spark

"You did it for money? You killed my sister for money?"

"And to stay out of prison," Colin states flatly. He stops pacing, and a smile slowly makes its way across his smug face. "But prison is no longer a problem for me now, is it? Tell me, Maddock, before I kill you, tell me what the feds know?"

"Fuck you!"

"I was hoping you'd say that." Colin turns and makes a hand signal to someone behind me. "Time to re-acquaint yourself with Mr. Black."

Scarface comes into my line of vision, smiling maniacally at me. He blows me a kiss. "Nothing I like better than getting people to talk, and I think I'm going to get you to sing for me, Maddock, like a fucking opera singer."

Rio walks into the room pushing a cart. He slows down as he gets to me ensuring I get a good look at the assortment of knives and other sharp instruments on there.

"The marshal who was looking after you, Styles? He was a tough cookie, his fucking heart gave out before I could get him to talk."

"Bullshit. He died in the line of duty," I say scathingly.

"Is that what they told you?" Laughs Rio.

"Guess the marshals wouldn't advertise the fact one of their own got taken. Bad for business," sneers Colin.

"You worthless piece of shit," I yell at Colin, straining against my restraints. "I *will* kill you!"

"Good luck. Gentlemen, let me know what you find out." Colin gives me one last smile and walks from the room.

I glare at my torturers. My heart is pounding, and I know I need to calm down. I have to find a way out of this before they carve me up. Rio and Black are grinning at me with jubilation, clearly excited with what they're about to do.

"Any last requests?" asks Black as he picks up one blade then another, holding it to the light.

"How about you stab Rio, then kill yourself? It'd make me happy," I reply with a grin.

"Your bravado is amusing. We shall see how long it lasts," Black says as he appears to be weighing a knife in his hand. "Mr. Lamond wants to know what you told the feds and if there's any written proof? He believes he's scrubbed his company clean, and it's why you haven't testified yet. He's successfully kept them at bay, and let's face it, without you, they have nothing."

It explains why I've been kept in the dark for so long, Maria's surprise visit, and the death of Marshal Styles.

Black walks toward me, eyes shining with excitement. "Rio, you may want to leave."

Rio gives me a sympathetic nod and heads for the door. Black puts the knife against my shoulder and slowly pushes it into me. Pain explodes with ferocity while I grit my teeth together to stop myself from screaming.

Closing my eyes, I let out a growl, and my mind wanders back to Cherie. I see her in her leather outfit with her head tilted to the side as she listens to my lies. I wish I had told her the truth. By now, it doesn't matter. She probably knows everything.

I feel him twist the knife, and as hard as I try, I'm unable to stop the roar that rips through me.

"They all break eventually," mutters Black.

I feel sweat build across my forehead. Opening my eyes, I glare at him. "I'm going to kill you!"

"Tut, tut, tut. They all say that, too." Black does a twirl, his hands held out away from his side. "As you can see, I'm still here." Chuckling, he picks up another knife and walks toward me. Black's voice becomes hard. "Tell me what I want to know, and this will end for you." He looks into my eyes as he plunges a knife into my other shoulder.

The pain is so extreme I feel sick, and blackness washes over me.

CHAPTER 17

Cherie

Sean is going so fast that I find it easier to close my eyes and hang on. We stop once on our journey to fill up with fuel.

"What's the plan?" I ask.

"We wait here for Angus. Then we head for Holly Airport. There's a guy there who owes us. He'll fly us to DC, no questions asked. It'll take us about three hours to get there, then it's only a matter of waiting."

Sean avoids eye contact. "It'll be too late, won't it?"

He nods and walks into the service station. When he returns, he hands me a chocolate bar. "Good for energy."

"Yeah, and my hips," I reply as I rip into it.

"A man likes a woman with meat on her."

Spark

I grin at him. "Might be true for some but not all."

Dismissively, he waves a hand at me. "The others aren't worth worrying about. A good woman will always be a good woman, no matter how big her ass is."

I laugh. "Such a sweet talker."

Sean arches an eyebrow at me. "Nope, telling it like it is." He points to a single headlight making its way down the highway. "Here comes Angus."

Angus pulls in and dismounts. "Do you ever turn on your fucking phone?"

"What's up your ass?"

"Kyle's been following Lamond. He thinks he might know where Maddock is. We don't need the girl anymore."

Both men look at me.

"Fuck you. I'm coming. I'll make my goddamn way home. But I am coming."

Sean grins, Angus shakes his head.

"She's coming, Angus. I like her. If Mad isn't interested, I think I might keep her."

"Sorry, big guy, *not* going to happen. But thank you for the... compliment?" I say, struggling for the right words.

"Fucking balls, man," says Sean as he lightly punches his brother's arm.

Not knowing what to make of either of them, I bite into my chocolate bar.

CHAPTER 18

Kyle

The warehouse they have my brother in is dark and abandoned. It's near the airport, and Lamond has left. I have three of my MC with me. My Sargeant-at-Arms, Wheels, who would never let me get into anything without him, is my best friend, and Rocky and Diesel are founding members of my MC.

We aren't a traditional MC. We are small compared to some, so most other MCs leave us alone. I split all the profits with my men. I get thirty percent, ten percent goes into an emergency fund and the taxman, and the remaining fifty percent gets divided amongst my brothers, depending on their involvement in the job or their standing in the MC. It works. We look after our own. No one goes hungry or poor.

"Want us to follow Lamond?" asks Rocky.

Spark

I shake my head. "Nah. Go around the back, che—"

A roar pierces the air, and I take a step toward the warehouse.

Wheels clamps a hand down on my shoulder. "Not so fast, Prez. We need to make sure we aren't going into a fuck-up." I scowl at him. "Fine, we're going in, but let's do it smartly. Send Rocky and Diesel around the back like you were going to do, and we'll move in the front."

I nod. "You're right. Let's do this quick. I haven't seen Maddock in over three years, and I'd rather not bury him a second time."

"We're on it. Give us five minutes to get around the back. We'll text when we're in position," says Diesel.

"Double-time it, yeah? 'Cause if I hear another noise, I'm going in."

Diesel doesn't answer, and they both jog away. I chose these men for this job as I know they will always have my back.

"Come on, Kyle, let's get a closer look. See what we can see." Wheels goes ahead of me.

All the windows are blacked out, so we can't see shit. Wheels pulls his Glock out of its holster and tries the handle on the door, slowly turning it. He looks tense, and sweat drips down his temple. Have you ever noticed when you are trying to be quiet, the smallest sound is amplified times a damn thousand?

He grimaces at me, but the door opens.

I nod, and we wait for the others to get into position.

CHAPTER 19

Maddock

A noxious smell wakes me, and pain radiates throughout my body. It takes me a moment to realize where I am. Mr. Black laughs and puts the smelling salts on the trolley.

"Not such a tough guy? Two little stab wounds, and you pass out like a pansy. I thought you'd be made of tougher stuff."

"Fuck. You," I grind out.

In response, he twists the knife in my shoulder. This time the sound which escapes my throat is a cross between a scream and a yell.

"I'm going to *kill* you," I shout.

"Again, with the meaningless threats... tsk, tsk, tsk." Black walks over and picks up another knife, points it at me, and grins. "Did you know, if done correctly, you can stab a person numerous times without killing them? I once stuck someone over fifty times. They eventually died from loss of blood as I nicked an artery, but I'm more careful now. Shall we see if you can break my record?"

"Fuck you, you sick fucker."

"Such language." He takes a step away from me, waving a hand in the air, then he stops and looks me in the eyes. "Do you have written proof?" Black asks casually.

"Of course, there's written proof," I yell.

"Who has it?"

"The feds. Who else do you think has it, fuckwit?"

"Liar, liar, pants on fire," sings Black. He picks up another knife which shines under the lights. Black smiles, strolls toward me, and drags it down the side of my face. Blood seeps into my eye, causing it to sting. I blink repeatedly. "All you have to tell me is the truth."

"You're going to kill me, anyway," I grind out.

"Yes, but it will be quick and humane." Black places the blade above my knee, letting it sink in. I feel it's tip bite into me through my jeans. "Do you have written proof?"

I clench my jaw together and glare at him.

"Which leg do you favor, the left or the right? Or should I pick?" Black's smile grows bigger, he pulls the knife away, chuckles, then he plunges it into my right leg above the knee.

Spark

The pain in my shoulders burns through me as I convulse at the pressure and pain I now feel. The sound that escapes me is more like a wounded animal, spittle sprays from my lips as I release my agony. Sweat and blood burn my eyes. I hear Black laughing as he enjoys my suffering. In my mind, I keep repeating that pain can be controlled, but as he twists the knife in my leg, I fear it is merely a useless mantra.

A loud bang sounds from behind me, and Black staggers back. Red spreads across his chest, and he's looking at me with a stupefied expression as though he's not comprehending what's happening to him. Black reaches down and touches the red. He's staring at his fingertips, locking eyes with me. He smiles, collapses to his knees, then falls face-first onto the concrete.

Kneeling in front of me, I see my brother, Kyle's face.

Hysterical laughter fills the room.

It takes me a moment to realize it's me.

Surely, this is another trick? Or I'm hallucinating?

"I've got you, brother," says the figment of my imagination who seems to resemble Kyle.

I shake my head as my laughter turns to tears. This can't be real. I've wanted this for far too long—to see my family, to hear their voices.

Black has finally pushed me over the edge.

Kyle pulls out a knife, and that's when I know he's not my brother.

"No," I yell at him.

Kyle uses the knife to cut my restraints. He reaches up, placing his hand behind my neck and places his forehead to mine. "You're home," whispers Kyle. "Look at my arm, Maddock, look at the ink that binds us."

It's a long-standing joke between us. Not only do we have blood, but the tattoo binds us as well.

I look at his arm and then lock eyes with him. "I'm sorry, brother," I whisper.

"Mad, you have nothing to be sorry for." Kyle nods at me and stands. "He's going to need medical attention. We can't move him. Do we know someone who can come here? Someone we can trust?"

I follow Kyle's stare and see Wheels, who gives me a chin lift. "Good to see you, Mad, but fuck, you look like shit. Yeah, Prez, I'm on it." Wheels walks a few paces away with his phone to his ear.

Panic rushes through me. I try to stand, but nothing works properly. "Kyle, there's another guy, there's another fucking guy!"

Kyle has his gun on his hand. He and Wheels head to the back of the warehouse, leaving me alone and worried for their safety. I can't move. The pain from trying to stand emanates throughout my entire body. The pain is so great, I feel like I'm going to vomit or pass out or probably both. The thought of blacking out steels my will to stay awake. I'm not safe, and my brother is somewhere in here with a psychopath.

Diesel walks toward me. "Fuck, brother, you've seen better days. Kyle sent me back here. Rocky and I knocked out a big black fucker. Are there any more?"

"N-No. Just him. Lamond was here."

"Yeah, we know, he's how we found you."

I peer up at Diesel and nod.

Pain shoots through me, and I'm thankfully transported into blackness.

CHAPTER 20

Cherie

We arrived at the clubhouse compound not long after Eric or Maddock arrived. Sean made it clear to everyone I was family and was to be treated like I'm precious. It's been a while since a man has treated me like that. And now I've found two in the same family. Whoever raised these men did it right.

A large man, who bears a striking resemblance to Sean and Maddock, strides toward me. He is fierce-looking, and he doesn't look happy. I stumble back a couple of paces, and he increases his speed. I feel like a rabbit caught in a trap, and I'm about to bolt when he's upon me. The man engulfs me in a bear hug, lifting me clean off the ground.

"I'm so happy to meet you. You mean something to my brother, so you mean something to me." He releases me and spreads his arms wide. "To us." I look beyond him, and the men behind him are grinning and nodding. The impression I have of an MC is entirely wrong if these men are anything to go by. "He's been asking for you." He places a hand on his chest. "I'm Kyle, this is the Loyal Rebels MC. You have nothing to fear here."

"Eric asked for me?"

"*Maddock* asked for you."

"Right, right. Where is he?" I ask impatiently.

Sean appears at my side, grabs my hand, and pulls me away from Kyle and the rest of the MC. "He's in and out of consciousness. He's asked for you a couple of times, but he's pretty groggy and in a lot of pain. You need to prepare yourself. He's hurt pretty bad."

I stop and gaze up at Sean. He locks eyes with me and opens the door with his other hand, pushing it wide. Sean reaches up with his fingers and brushes the hair from my face.

"You need anything, you call me." Sean's thumb rubs across my cheek, and it sends shivers through me.

"Cherie?" whispers Eric.

Breaking out of Sean's grip, I hurry to Eric, grasping his hand. "Hey, Eric, are you okay?"

Eric has a sheet over his body and bandages over both shoulders. Blood has seeped through the white gauze fabric. His face is badly bruised, and he has a black eye. The room looks like something out of a hospital. It feels like a surgical room—sterile, clean—not a room in an MC clubhouse.

"I am now, and it's Maddock. Thanks for coming."

"Well, your brothers have taken good care of me."

A look passes across his face, and he looks past me to Sean. "I'm sure he has."

I frown down at him and touch his face. "For someone who lied to me about everything, you're kinda cocky. Your family is pretty tight." Maddock nods and winces. "Are you in pain?" I ask worriedly.

"Only when I breathe."

"Do you want me to get the doctor?" asks Sean as he comes into the room, placing a hand on my shoulder as he does.

"Yeah, Sean, that would be good."

I watch Sean leave, and my gaze goes back to Maddock, who's staring at me. "He's been amazing. Sean and Angus brought me to you here in DC. They've been nothing but nice to me."

"I'm sure they have." The tone in his voice is full of sarcasm.

"Is that supposed to mean something? Your brothers have told me more truth about you in the short space of time I've known them than you have the whole time I've known you. And let's not forget, I came hundreds of miles for *you*."

Spark

Maddock's face softens. "I'm sorry I didn't tell you the truth, and I'm glad you're here."

"It's been interesting," I say with a chuckle.

Sean comes back into the room with a man. I take a step back so they can work on Maddock.

"On a scale of one to ten, one being the best, ten being the worst, how's your pain?" asks the man I assume is the doctor.

"I'm at an eight."

"Okay, I'm going to give you something, but you're going to go to sleep pretty quickly."

The doctor goes to a cabinet on the wall, opens it, and pushes a syringe into a vial. He quirks an eyebrow at me. "If there's something you want to say to him, now's the time."

I move back to Maddock, lean over, and kiss his forehead. "I'll be here when you wake up. Sweet dreams."

"Only of you."

I laugh and nod. "See you in your dreams."

Sean guides me from the room. "What do you want to do?" he asks.

"I'd kill for a hot shower and a meal."

Sean grabs my hand. "Your wish is my command. Come with me." He leads me down a long hallway and into a room. "This is my space. You'll find a shower behind door number one. If you give me your clothes, I'll get them cleaned."

"You know someone who can clean leather pants?"

Sean laughs. "I'll figure it out." He moves past me and opens a closet, pulling out some tracksuit pants and a black T-shirt. Sean holds them up. "Will these do until I get your clothes cleaned?"

"Perfect! And thank you."

"You need any help getting out of those pants?" Sean asks as I take the clothes off him.

"I'm good."

"Okay then, drop them outside the bathroom door, and I'll take care of them. And shout if you need anything, and I do mean anything," says Sean with a smirk.

I grin at him, shake my head, and close the bathroom door.

As I lean up against it, relief washes over me, knowing Eric is okay. But he did lie to me. And now I'm miles away from my home with a bunch of men I don't know.

Hell, do I really know Eric? Maddock?

Jesus! I sure can pick them.

CHAPTER 21

Sean

Damn! If this woman isn't the sexiest, ballsiest woman I've met in a long time. The only downside is it's obvious she's into my brother. My brother, who I thought was dead, the brother who is lying in our surgical suite cut up to all hell. I wait outside my room until I hear the shower start, then I go in and pick her clothes up off the floor. She's hung her jacket on the back of the door, so I'm guessing it doesn't need cleaning.

Kyle meets me in the hallway. "How is she?"

"Cherie is cool. Taking a shower."

"You like her?"

"What's not to like?"

"She's your brother's girl. Come on, Sean, use your head."

"He's lied to her. And I'm pretty sure he hasn't staked a claim. Far as I can tell, she's fair game," I say with a nod and a smirk.

Kyle glares at me and places a hand on his hip. It's something he does when he's angry, and if he's really angry, he cocks an eyebrow too. "Sean, as my VP, I'm telling you to back off. Not only because he's our brother but because it's the right thing to do."

A part of me knows what Kyle is saying is true, but I can't deny the attraction I feel for Cherie.

"How about we let her decide, yeah? As for Maddock, have we asked him about Heather yet? And are Jamie and Loch on their way here?" I ask Sean, trying to distract him.

He frowns. "No, I haven't asked him about Heather. Loch and Jamie are on their way. I didn't tell them why, only that it was important that they come here. You know how Jamie is. I basically told him it was a matter of life and death. Since Maddock died, he's been keeping away from us... from the MC. I think he thinks it was my fault."

"Yeah, Jamie is going to be pissed. He blamed you, us, because of that dick detective. He said it was probably connected to the MC. Maybe now we can rebuild our family. All we need is Heather," I reply quietly.

"If she's alive. It doesn't make sense for them to put her into witness protection. Angus has found a mountain of stuff on Zed Fluid Systems. Heather had nothing to do with it." Kyle drops his hand from his hip and scrubs it across his face.

"Gotta have a little faith, brother. After all, Maddock has come back to us."

Kyle nods, but his face is grim. He won't allow himself to believe Heather could be alive. I know him all too well. For him, it would be like losing her all over again. For me, once Angus found snippets of proof that Maddock was alive, I've clung to the hope, Heather is too. I won't give up on her. She was the best of us.

It's been three hours since Maddock was given pain relief and drifted off to sleep. Cherie has been fed and is now sitting across from me in the clubhouse bar. She looks good in my clothes. The pants are rolled up, and I gave her a pair of socks to wear. Cherie is sitting with one leg tucked under her, and the other is bent up on the chair with her hands folded over her knee. She looks comfortable, at ease.

"So what do you think of DC?" I ask.

"Anything's better than a small town," Cherie responds.

"You don't like living in the country?"

"I like living in Breckenridge for my granddaddy. It's always been home, but it's not the place I want to spend the rest of my days. The world is a big place, and I hope to see it all one day." She looks wistful as she talks about her plans.

"Did Maddock ever tell you about us?"

Cherie looks surprised, her leg drops to the floor, and she leans forward. "He was very cryptic, at least now I know why. Do you know how he came to be in witness protection?"

"Angus has gathered information regarding the company he worked for, Zed Fluid Systems, but we'd need to confirm it with Mad."

"I gather Angus is something of a computer genius? How does he find the information?"

I raise my hands in the air. "I have no idea. I can barely use my phone properly. Angus has always had a knack with electronics and computers. I'm more of a muscle man."

Cherie grins at me. "All brawn, no brain?"

I scoff at her. "Nice!"

"I didn't mean it. We're all good at something."

"I'm good with my hands, weapons, explosives—"

"Explosives! What on earth?"

"I was in the Marines. Joined up straight out of school."

"Ahh, makes sense."

Spark

"So tell me, Cherie, what are you good at?" I tease her.

Her face clouds over. "I don't know yet, unless waitressing counts?"

"I bet you're good at a lot of things," I say as I give her the once over. To my surprise, Cherie blushes and looks down. "You look good in my T-shirt, it suits you. If you wanted to stay—"

"Sean, Cherie… Maddock's awake and wants to see you." It's Kyle, and his timing is perfect.

I scowl at him as Cherie and I both stand. "Lead the way, *brother*," I growl.

Kyle raises his eyebrows at me and gives a small shake of his head. I need to be careful. Kyle is my brother first and foremost, but he's also the head of our MC. He won't stand for any kind of insubordination. He rules with an iron fist.

We follow him to the surgical suite, and Maddock is sitting up, waiting for us.

"How are you feeling?" asks Cherie as she takes a seat next to his bed.

"Better," replies Maddock as he reaches for her hand. He holds eye contact with her for a moment, then looks to me. "Are Loch and Jamie here?"

"How'd you know we'd summoned them?" asks Kyle.

"Angus. He's been in and out of here ever since you brought me here. The clubhouse has certainly had some upgrades since I was here last."

"That's what happens when you disappear for three goddamn years," I say a little more forcefully than I intended, but seeing the way Cherie is looking at him and his reaction to her, it pisses me off.

"It's a long story, Sean, and I want to tell it but not until the others are here. I want to say this once and answer all the questions. Brother, I thought I was protecting all of you."

I can see the sincerity in his eyes. I've let the woman cloud my judgment. Nodding, I head for the door, only to have Kyle place an arm across the doorway blocking me.

"Don't go far."

"I'm not, Prez. Going to check how far away the others are." Something goes across Kyle's face at the sound of me calling him Prez.

He nods once and punches me lightly on the arm. "Good idea."

I head back out into the bar area, scanning the room. Diesel and Rocky motion for me to come over.

"Hey, VP, how's he doing?" asks Diesel.

"He's awake. He's a tough son of a bitch. Any word on how far away Jamie and Lochlan are?"

Our family founded this MC. The members know all of us, even those who are not strictly part of it. Kyle has always made a point of getting to know all the families of the brotherhood. As president, he's

Spark

made it a point to find out about all of them, to understand them, and to know who can be trusted. Your family says a lot about you and your ability to walk away from them or bring them into the fold speaks volumes about who you are as a person.

"They should be here by now. Can't be too far away," replies Rocky.

"Beer?" asks Diesel.

"Got something stronger?"

"Whiskey?"

"Now, we're talking." Diesel grins at me and walks toward the bar.

The doors to the clubhouse open, and I look up to see Jamie and Loch walk through them. Jamie has curly red hair and is dressed in jeans and a flannel shirt. Loch is tall, well-built, and wearing a suit. You can see they are brothers but from different worlds. Jamie's hair is a mess, and Lochlan's is neatly combed. When their eyes lock with mine they both smile.

"About time you sorry sons of bitches got here," I bellow at them.

"I was told it was a matter of life and death, so I'm here," says Jamie pragmatically. He's always been the practical one, but after the death of Maddock and Heather, he withdrew from us. It didn't matter that I could prove the MC didn't have anything to do with their deaths, he always thought we played a hand in it.

"It's good to see you, brother."

Jamie nods, and the smile is gone. It's clear he wants to hear what we have to say and go back to the farm. Lochlan gives me a bear hug, lifting me from the floor.

"Whoa, little brother. You're stronger than you look."

"Weights, bro, weights. The ladies love muscles, and so do the men."

"Fuck that," I say as he drops me.

"It pays the bills." Lochlan takes a step back and grins.

"Heard you were dating some supermodel or some shit?" asks Diesel as he hands me a whiskey.

"For a while." Lochlan looks around and stares back at me. "Why were we summoned? I've got work in Paris I need to get back to."

"Is that what the cool kids call it now?" Diesel smirks.

"Why are we here, Sean? Loch isn't the only one who has things to do. I have a farm to run."

"We know." I throw back my whiskey and walk away from them. "Follow me."

I don't turn around, I know they're behind me. I pause at the door, hand resting on the front of it. "You need to prepare yourselves." I glance over my shoulder at them. Jamie looks annoyed and Loch slightly bored. Pushing open the door, I go through first.

Spark

Jamie walks in, eyes wide open in disbelief. "Maddock, is that you? Is Heather here?" His eyes dart all around the room taking in everything and searching for our sister.

"No, Heather is gone. I felt her leave," replies Lochlan in a whisper. "How did you survive? Angus has been saying you're still alive but..."

It was hardest on Loch as he was Heather's twin. They were inseparable when they were kids, even had their own language. His eyes are filled with tears as he stares at Maddock.

"No, Heather is dead. I'm so sorry if any of you thought she was still here with us," whispers Maddock.

Jamie closes the gap between them, dragging Maddock into an awkward embrace. Mad draws in a ragged breath, and from the look on his face, he must be in agony, but he doesn't push Jamie away.

Cherie stands and whispers something to Jamie I can't hear. He leans back to look at Maddock, nods, and gently releases him. Before she sits back down, she sweeps the hair off Maddock's face, and with that one gesture, I know she could never be mine.

"Where's Angus? We shouldn't start this without him," says Kyle as he drags a chair closer to the bed.

"I'll go find him." I cast one more look at Cherie and gladly leave that room.

CHAPTER 22

Maddock

Here I am surrounded by family and Cherie. I've wanted this for so long, and now I have to confess how I got my sister killed. How I trusted the wrong people and my stupidity got the one good thing in this family extinguished.

Cherie stands and is heading for the door.

"Where are you going?" I ask.

She stops and turns around. "This is clearly a family matter, and I—"

"Stay," orders Kyle.

"You showed up and have looked after him. It's all we could want. You get to stay," says Sean, shocking me with his honesty.

Although I don't like the way my brother is looking at her. I might have been away for a long time, but I know my brother. Sean likes Cherie, and with my dishonesty, she might be interested in him. She told me from the get-go not to be a jerk.

Cherie looks at the others, and they nod. She returns to her chair, and I take her hand in mine.

"This is Cherie," I say as I hold up our hands, making it clear she's mine. "She was about my only friend I had in the town I was living in." I raise her hand to my lips and kiss it lightly, then I turn and look at my brothers. "I discovered Zed Fluid Systems was selling parts through a shell corporation to some groups in Iran. These parts could potentially be used to make dirty bombs. I told Colin Lamond, he's the CEO of the company. I thought he was unaware of the activity. I was wrong. That's what got Heather and almost me, killed."

"Why was Heather at your house?" asks Lochlan. He's standing stiffly in the corner, arms wrapped around himself.

"It was her car. It was making a noise. Heather turned up, and I told her to take mine, said I'd take the bike and look at the car when I got home. It was the morning after I told Lamond about the discrepancies I found in accounting. The FBI was already investigating the company, so they convinced me to go into witness protection. They told me I needed to protect all of you. To play dead. I'm so sorry..." I'm looking at my fingers entwined with Cherie's, and no one in the room makes a sound. "I know it couldn't have been easy to bury both of us. The emotional toll on all of you must have been horrible." I look up searching my family's faces. "I honestly thought it was the right thing to do."

Loch scrubs a hand over his face. Sean is looking at the floor, his body is taut, his face is a mask of anger.

"I knew you were still alive. Witness protection leaves fingerprints on everything *if* you know where to look. I hoped Heather was still with us, but I couldn't find anything on her, not a damn thing. Now, at least we know for sure," Angus discloses with a thick voice.

Loch stalks out of the room with Kyle hot on his heels.

I look at Sean questioningly.

"You gotta know, Mad, he'd take this harder than all of us."

"Fuck that! *You* should have found a fucking way to let us know you were alive. All this goddamn time I've been mourning *you*, I've been blaming Kyle and Sean *and* this fucking MC. I-I've been…"

Sean rises and embraces Jamie. The anger pouring out of him is palpable in the room. Jamie has always been the glue keeping the family together. It's hard to believe he turned his back on them because of me.

"Jamie, I was told again and again I was keeping you safe. I had to believe it. You have to know the only thing I wanted was to come home. To see all of you."

"We have to let them know where you are," states Angus.

Jamie looks at Angus. "Who?"

"Law enforcement, the Feds, somebody," answers Angus.

"Fuck that," replies Sean.

"If we don't, Lamond will walk. Maddock is the only proof they have. He *has* to go back," states Angus emphatically.

"Not unless you get the dirt on Lamond." All eyes go to Cherie. "Well, it's true, right? Maddock won't have to testify if we can get Lamond to confess or at least incriminate himself."

Sean grins at her. Angus nods.

"Whatever you two are thinking, *no*. I'll go back. I'll testify," I say as I try to sit up a bit further. Pain courses through my shoulders and stops me from any further movement.

"That's why we need to do this. What if they come after us next time? It'd be easy enough to drive a truck over Sean or Kyle," states Angus.

Sean looks him up and down. "Thanks, brother. Have I told you I don't like the way you think?"

"Listen to me. All we need to do is get Lamond on tape or something. How hard can it be?"

"Right! Like the FBI haven't been trying for years," bellows Sean.

"The guy who tortured me, he said they have the FBI in their pocket, so this may be the reason why they've never managed to get anything on him."

Angus looks down at the floor. From my bed, I can see his mind working. It's in his stance and the grim determination on his face.

"He like women?" asks Angus.

"Yeah, he does or did. Why?" I ask.

Angus looks at Cherie. "She could be our decoy. Cherie could go home with him, drug him, and I could tap his phones, bug his home. Easy, simple."

"Fuck, no! Cherie *isn't* going anywhere near him. Are we clear?" I growl.

Cherie stands. "Everybody out! No one comes back in here until I say so. Are *we* clear?"

Angus and Jamie appear shocked, but Sean looks like the cat who swallowed the canary.

"Big brass balls, that's what she's got." Sean looks me in the eyes and points at me. "You don't claim this one, I will. Come on, you two, let's leave them alone. Something tells me the lady has a lot to say." Sean winks at Cherie as she ushers them out of the room.

Cherie locks the door and leans up against it with a smile on her face.

"Is there something you want to tell me about you and my brother?" I ask.

Cherie looks taken aback. "What?"

"I see the way he looks at you."

"Un-fucking-believable!" Cherie yells, putting her hands on her hips as she strides toward me. "I travel here, with *your* brothers, the brothers I knew nothing, absolutely nothing about, for *you*! And this is how you treat me? Jesus, Eric! No, wait, it's Maddock, isn't it?"

Her outburst makes me ashamed of myself, but damn, if she isn't the sexiest woman alive.

"You're right, I'm sorry."

"And…" her hands drop from her hips. "Wait, I'm right?"

"Yes, you're right. I'm a dick. I see the way he looks at you and…"

"Do you see the way *I* look at you?" Cherie whispers.

Slowly, she walks toward me. I'm at a loss for words, unsure of her next move or what she wants or needs from me.

"How's your leg?"

"It's okay, not as bad as my shoulders."

Her change of conversation has me confused.

"Can you handle a little pressure?"

"I'm not sure…"

In one swift movement, Cherie gets on the bed and straddles me. "How does it feel?" she asks as she grinds into me.

"Like one of us has too many clothes on."

I have a sheet over my body, and apart from bandages, I'm naked. Cherie, on the other hand, has on a T-shirt and tracksuit pants. I reach up and touch her face, but it causes pain to shoot through me. Grasping my hand, Cherie puts it on the bed next to her leg.

"Lover, I can do everything. I only need you to lie there. Can you do that for me?"

My cock responds instantly when her lips press up against mine. It's a slow, burning kiss which sparks a fire within me. My hands go to her ass, and I move her, and she responds by groaning into my mouth. Her tongue darts in and out causing me to groan. I want more. I want to consume her.

"Wait, wait, wait. How are you feeling?"

"Babe, if you can't feel how I'm doing, then we're in trouble."

"No, I mean your pain levels. How are they?"

"Tell you what… let's get you naked and see what happens?"

"I don't want to hurt you," she whispers as she bites lightly on my earlobe.

"Blue balls would hurt me." I chuckle.

In response, she reaches down and pulls her T-shirt up over her head, exposing her breasts. Leaning forward, I draw one of her nipples into my mouth. Her moan and the way she grinds into me is the only encouragement I need.

I reach up to press her closer to me, and instead of a groan of pleasure, pain shoots down my body, and I yelp in agony.

Cherie sits back, looking apprehensive. "Okay, this was a bad idea." She climbs off me, and I am powerless to stop her.

"Babe, no way. We need to be a bit more careful, that's all, and that was all on me."

"We can wait till you feel better. Can't we?"

Reluctantly, I nod my head. "Yeah, we can."

Cherie's face flushes. "Let's talk about Angus' plan."

"No," I say, flatly.

"Lover, if I can help, I want to."

"It's too dangerous. They've tried to kill me once, and in doing so, they killed Heather. I can't let anything happen to you."

Cherie nods and puts her top back on. I realize it must be Sean's, and I scowl at her.

"Angus or Sean or one of your brothers will be there to protect me. It's not like I'm going to be in danger. All I have to do is drug him, and they'll do the rest."

"Is that Sean's tee?"

Cherie looks down and nods. "Yeah, I was still in my leathers. He offered to get them cleaned."

"I bet he did," I state roughly.

Cherie's eyes sparkle. "You're not jealous of your brother, are you? That's, well, that's ridiculous."

"You're wearing his clothes."

"And not two minutes ago I was trying to make love to you. Besides, we were talking about getting evidence, not an imaginary relationship between Sean and me. I want you, only you."

I close my eyes. I'm not sure who to thank for bringing her into my life, but I know someone sent her to me.

"Sorry, I'm an ass."

"Yes, you are." Cherie grins at me. "This plan could work, but I won't do it unless you say yes."

Before I can answer, the door opens, and Angus walks through. We both look at him in surprise.

"I picked the lock," explains Angus as he shrugs and sits on the end of the bed pushing his glasses up his nose. "We'll keep her safe. If things go sideways, we'll shoot his ass."

I glare at him, not happy with his intrusion and the fact he wants to put my woman in danger.

"No." I'm angry, and both of them turn to look at me with confusion on their faces. "I'm not putting Cherie in any danger. I'm not... repeat, I'm *not...* losing her."

"Er... Maddock, don't you see this is the only way we can stop them for good? Honey, you'll never be able to have a normal life if we don't do this."

"She's right, Mad," agrees Angus.

Spark

"They killed a U.S. Marshal. You think they'll even hesitate before they pull the trigger? It's too dangerous."

Cherie and Angus exchange a look.

I know I've lost.

"You really think your brothers can't take care of me? Honey, I'm practically *in* the MC. All I'd need to do is some form of initiation, and I'm sure Kyle would sign off."

This causes Angus and me to laugh, which causes pain to shoot throughout my body. In the end, it's a cross between laughing and groaning for me with Angus laughing harder at me.

I turn to look at her, and she's stone-cold serious, no trace of humor anywhere on her gorgeous face. It's like throwing a bucket of ice water in my face.

I stop.

I sigh in frustration. "What if something happens to you? What if I get you killed, too?"

From the doorway, Sean says, "We won't let that happen. We'll keep her safe. She's precious. No one is laying a finger on her."

I glance up at Cherie, and her face has gone all soft at Sean's words. Instinctively, I reach out and grab her hand. Cherie's eyes find mine, and she smiles. I tug on her hand, and she sits beside me, draping an arm behind my head. I look back at Sean and smile at him, letting him know she's mine. For a moment, he looks thunderous, and then he shakes himself and moves further into the room.

Smirking, Sean says, "We'll wire her. I'll do it personally so no one can find it."

"Like fuck, you will." I sit up straighter causing my body to protest with sharp pain, but I keep a lid on it and glare at him.

"Will you two stop it?" asks Cherie. "Honestly, this isn't high school. Angus can wire me up in this room with *you* watching."

Now it's my turn to smirk at Sean, who is looking at my woman like she could walk on water. I've never seen him look so reverently at any woman, although I haven't seen him in three years. I guess we've all changed.

"Sean, you give me your word Cherie will be safe, and I'll agree."

"On my life."

With those three words, I nod.

Cherie grabs my head, pulling me closer to her and kisses the side of it.

"I don't know if he still visits there, but Lamond used to frequent an exclusive gentleman's club on Sixteenth Street. Hell, I don't know if it even exists anymore," I say as my brothers filter into the room.

"It's still there. I can get her in," states Lochlan. His eyes are red-rimmed, and he holds my gaze. "Being an international model gets me in almost anywhere. I'll get my agent to contact the club. It should be easy." Lochlan's gaze moves to Cherie. "I'll need to bring another woman with me, so it looks like I'm ignoring you. That way you can sit at the bar and try and catch Lamond's eye."

"I don't know anyone here," replies Cherie.

Lochlan smiles. "It's okay, I have a few female friends I can count on."

"I need to go shopping," states Cherie.

"I'll take you." Sean steps forward, grinning.

"No, you won't. It has to be Loch or someone not affiliated with the club. The minute Lamond finds out you're not at the warehouse, he'll be on alert," says Kyle with authority. "Hell, he might not even come out to play."

"Have you got people on the warehouse where I was being kept?"

"Yeah, no one's gone in yet. It's risky, but we were thinking we could get your friend, Rio, to phone him and set up a meet at the club."

It's a good plan *if* Lamond takes the bait. All we need to do is get Rio to go along with it. I'm thinking he wants out of the pit we've dropped him in, so he shouldn't need too much persuasion.

I look at Lochlan. "Does he know you're my brother?"

"Yes, but it's not unusual for me to be in DC or for me to be in exclusive clubs. I'm friends with Colton Anders, quarterback for the New England Warriors. He's in town tonight. I'll ask him to join us." Loch glances at Cherie. "He's a player, he's good-looking, cocky, and you're so his type."

"I know who Colt Anders is. Hell, every woman in the United States knows who he is."

"Loch…" I begin to say.

"I'll tell him I'm bringing some women with me, which means now I need three, and I'll tell him Cherie is off-limits. You okay with getting your picture in the paper?" Loch asks Cherie.

"Why?"

"Honey, I'm one of the leading faces for romantic book covers, and that's beside my contracts with Chanel and Armani. Colton is a bonafide football hero, and the press follows him around like flies."

"So my picture might end up in a magazine?" asks Cherie, smiling.

"Yes, and the newspapers. Might even end up on television with 'Who's That Girl?'. Everyone will want to know who you are."

"I like the sound of that."

"I don't," I say flatly.

"Aww, honey, I'm thinking about all those small-minded people back home. Can you imagine the gossip that's going to be floating around about me if I'm seen with Colton Anders?"

"You know I *am* famous," states Loch with a hint of irritation.

Cherie smiles. "Okay, who's taking me shopping?"

Loch holds up a hand. "I'm going to call Miranda Tuturo. She owes me. That way you'll look like arm candy tonight and not a potential girlfriend. If Lamond is paying attention to us, you'll look like the next 'it' girl. No one important."

"Someone needs to be close to Cherie while she's shopping. She needs to be safe," I interject.

"I'll get a prospect, someone new to the club to escort her," says Kyle.

"Someone who looks pretty," replies Lochlan with a grin.

"Fuck if I know who looks pretty. Go and look around the club. You know all the long-standing members, so pick someone you don't know."

Loch nods and moves out. Cherie stands, her hand firmly held in mine. I look at the people in the room—all eyes are on Cherie. Although I have my reservations about this plan, I know the men in this room will keep my woman safe.

CHAPTER 23

Cherie

I'm sitting in an exclusive boutique with a young biker who was forced to wear a long-sleeve shirt and dress pants. His name is Moose as he's as big as one, and he looks about as comfortable as a biker can look when he's out of his element.

I smile at him, and he sort of grimaces at me. He didn't want this detail, but Kyle insisted he come. Lochlan picked him as he could pass for a normal guy, but with the way he's acting, he's not fooling anyone.

"Madame, we selected some dresses for you. Your friend..." the man nods toward Miranda, "... Ms. Tuturo, suggested would be acceptable for tonight. Now, if you'd come this way?" replies the boutique owner gesturing toward the fitting rooms. He's a middle-aged man with lots of flair, and he's

Spark

kept an eye on Moose the entire time he has been in the front of the boutique.

I glance up at Moose as he takes two steps toward me.

"Of course your bodyguard may come, too," purrs the owner as he looks Moose up and down in a pleasing way.

Moose glares at him.

"I'm sure my associate could wait here. After all, I'm only behind the curtain."

Moose walks past all of us and goes into the dressing rooms. He returns a short time later and nods at me. The owner looks like he could eat him alive. Moose takes my seat and faces the curtain to the dressing room, avoiding everyone's gaze.

Miranda smirks at me, and we both go behind the curtain.

"I think you would look good in all of these, but..." she holds one up, "... this one will show off your curves to the best advantage."

It's a little black dress, emphasis on *little*. I frown slightly, take off my clothes, and slip on the dress. Miranda zips me up and then holds my hair up off my face.

"Hmm... no, you look better with your hair down. You have such gorgeous hair."

"Thank you."

Miranda waves a hand at me. "Go show Moose, let's see what he thinks."

I open the curtain and walk out. Moose's eyes are on the floor, his gaze travels up my body, and he slowly rises to his feet, adjusting himself as he does. "Damn," he whispers.

"So it looks okay?" I ask.

Miranda bursts out laughing. "That, darling, is a definite yes."

I look at her sideways, then back at Moose who is nodding, all while the shop owner is looking at Moose, his expression one of exasperation at Moose's obvious attraction to me.

I turn and go back behind the curtain. Miranda unzips me, and I try on all of the dresses one by one, but the first one is the winner.

Miranda helps me choose shoes and an evening bag, all the while the boutique owner looks longingly at Moose who's doing his best to ignore him and scan for potential threats which, of course, there are none.

"Why are you smiling?" asks Miranda.

"I get to be a princess for a day. What's not to be happy about?"

"Ahh, you've never had this type of experience before?"

I laugh. "No, Miranda. I normally buy my clothes at discount or department stores, *not* boutiques. This whole experience is amazing."

Miranda nods and smiles the way you would at an indulgent child. "I see. Then let's go for the full

Spark

treatment... hair, tan, makeup. Let's make a day of it." She links her arm through mine, hands off the shopping bags to Moose, who looks up at the ceiling and groans.

We walk about two blocks, and Miranda takes me into the most expensive hair salon I've ever seen. Crystal chandeliers hang from the ceiling, and the chairs near the basins are the ones that massage. The owner is a woman who looks like she stepped out of a fashion magazine.

"Miranda! Darling! What on earth are you doing here?" gushes the owner as she hugs and kisses Miranda on both cheeks.

"Oh, I'm here with Lochlan, and this..." Miranda links an arm around this woman and waves a hand at me, "... is Cherie. I want you to... make her better."

"Hmm?" The owner breaks away from Miranda and grips my face, twisting it from side to side. "There is potential here." The owner looks over her shoulder at Miranda. "Can we do the works?"

"Yes."

"The works?" I whisper.

The owner steps back in her red, six-inch shiny heels. "I'm Ursula. I am going to transform you."

"We're keeping her hair, but the rest is up to you," states Miranda.

"Ahh, shouldn't I get a say?"

Ursula and Miranda laugh. "Oh, darling, when I'm done with you, you won't recognize yourself.

Now, let's take you into one of the back rooms so we can get you ready."

With that, I am whisked away, and my transformation begins.

Oh my God!

I'm sitting in the back of a limousine with Colton Anders, and he's smiling at *me*.

Lochlan is giving him the evil eye as I try and calm down my inner fangirl. Loch is nothing like his brothers. They look similar, but where Maddock is ruggedly handsome, Loch is more refined with slightly higher cheekbones, fuller lips, and his hair is trained into submission. There are three other women in the back with us, and to be fair, Colton is smiling at all of us. I'm wearing the little black dress with shoe-string straps and plunging back, my six-inch silver heels are killing my feet, but damn, I look good.

Even in his incapacitated state, Maddock looked like he could eat me alive. Miranda's friend, Ursula, was true to her word. They waxed every inch of me, spray-tanned me, painted my nails, did my makeup, gave my hair a trim, and styled it. I almost didn't recognize myself in the mirror. I feel pretty and sexy as hell.

Spark

"Remember, look bored when we get in there, pouty even, while Colt and I ignore you. Go sit at the bar, smile at Lamond but let him come to you," reminds Lochlan for the hundredth time.

"I know, we've been over thi—"

"Yes, we have. Mad would have my balls in a vice if anything happened to you, so play it safe."

"Or she could stay with us, and I could... entertain her all night long," teases Colt.

"You so much as look at her the wrong way, and my brothers will fuck you up, Colt. She's spoken for."

"Hello! In the car with you, you know?" I say sarcastically.

Miranda lets out a bored sigh. "I'll second that. You had better entertain *all* of us."

Colt's eyes go to the gorgeous Miranda, who is exotic looking. She has dark, flawless skin, legs that go on forever, and long, straight dark hair. Miranda is wearing a gold shoe-string dress which shows off her curves and makes her stand out in any crowd. She's a woman who knows how to make every man in the room want her, and she knows exactly how to use her sexuality to get what she wants. With the way Colton is now looking at her, I feel like the poor stepsister.

"Okay, here we are. You're on Colt's arm with the lovely Trinity. Miranda, you and Amity are with *me*." There's an edge to his voice as he glares at

Miranda who simply shrugs, but when Lochlan gets out of the car, she smiles and winks at me. Clearly, she's trying to make him jealous.

Colt steps out and helps Trinity exit the limousine first, then me. I'm unprepared for the flash of cameras as paparazzi begin yelling out questions to Colt and Loch.

Loch smiles at the camera, flanked by Miranda and Amity who pose like the supermodels they are. I hold my head up high and copy them as I take Colt's arm.

"Colt! Colt! Over here."

Our little trio turns around as Colt smiles for one of the hoard.

"Hello, Mickey. How's tricks?" asks Colt.

"Good, good..." Mickey is clicking away as he answers. "So, who are the lovely ladies?"

Colt gestures toward Trinity. "I'm sure you know Trinity Hernadez from the Ford Modeling Agency, and this exceptional beauty is Cherie Lake, the next big thing." Colt smiles and completely takes me by surprise by kissing me on the lips. He pulls back, growls at me, and winks at Mickey.

"Next big thing for you?" asks Mickey.

"You never know," replies Colt as he shepherds us into the club.

Once inside, Loch gives Colt a hard smile. "What the fuck was that?"

"Come on, Loch. She's gorgeous, and it was only a peck. The reporters are going to love it."

"My brother isn't," Loch states flatly.

Colt shrugs and winks at me. "Okay, okay, let's get a table, so I can start ignoring Cherie and give Trinity all my attention.

And just like that, Colt turns all his charms on Trinity, who looks like the cat who swallowed the canary. We make our way to a booth, and I'm positioned on the end nearest the aisle. After about fifteen minutes of sitting there as the guys and girls ignore me, Loch nods, and it's my cue to leave. I stand, look down at them, shake my head, and walk toward the bar.

More than one man follows my path with his eyes as I sit on a barstool, trying not to flash the room as I do. Lamond is across the room, and as I sit down, I smile at him, then look to the bartender for a drink.

"What'll be?"

Maddock told me what Lamond likes to drink. "Whiskey sour, please."

The bartender nods, and as I'm about to pay for it, a hand closes over mine and says, "Allow me."

It's Lamond, and he leers at me as he hands over his credit card.

"Well, thank you," I purr.

"Whiskey sour? Beautiful *and* tasteful. I'm Colin Lamond." He holds out his hand.

"Cherie." I grasp his hand in mine and smile.

He's in his late fifties, trim, going gray at the temples but still a vigorous-looking man.

"You came in with Colton Anders?"

I scoff. "Yeah, I *did*." Making it clear I'm no longer with him.

"Ahh, well, his loss is *my* gain." I smile seductively at him. "So, Cherie, what brings you to DC?"

Thankfully, Miranda has prepped me. "I'm here for the Chanel photoshoot. There's a group of us. I'm one of the many trying to stand out. My agent says they *are* interested in me for further campaigns, so I thought being seen with Colt might raise my profile, but he's more interested in Trinity."

Lamond looks over at the booth. They are all laughing and having a good time.

"He's a fool, and if you need a better agent, I know some people."

"Really?" I ask eagerly.

"Oh yeah, someone as beautiful as you shouldn't need to sully herself with a *football player*," sneers Lamond.

I give him my best smile and take a sip of my drink. It is awful, and it takes all my effort not to cough and choke on it.

Spark

Lamond holds out his hand. I place mine in his, and he leads me to a booth away from Lochlan on the other side of the room

"Do you come here often?" I ask as I slide onto the seat, and he does the same, sitting right next to me. This is nothing like the date I had with Maddock. I know who this man is, and he makes my skin crawl.

"Sometimes. A business associate wanted to meet me here, but he hasn't arrived." Colin pauses and looks around the room. His gaze comes back to me, and he smiles. "How long are you in DC for?"

Lamond twists and faces me, one of his hands lightly touches my shoulder, stroking back and forth. "Only until the end of next week. If Chanel wants me to continue with them, next week we'll be in New York, then Paris."

"Have you modeled for long?"

"Since I was twelve."

His eyes widen, and he leans in. "Is it true what they say about models?"

"Depends on what they say." As I say this, I lean into him and place a hand on his knee.

Lamond smiles, and his hand is now on my shoulder with his thumb making lazy circles on my skin. "It's supposed to be a very sexually active business, yes?"

"Depends on the photographer," I reply candidly.

"Want to get out of here?" he asks.

"Where shall we go?"

Lamond licks his lips and moves in closer, his other hand goes up my leg and stops at my waist. "I don't live far from here, and I have a jacuzzi. We could... get wet."

His hand travels back down my body, and he moves in and kisses me. His tongue forces itself into my mouth.

I place my hands on his chest and push him back, then smile seductively at him.

"Lead the way, tiger."

The trip to Lamond's house takes about twenty minutes, and his hand keeps traveling up and down my leg. Try as I might, I can't get him to keep both hands on the wheel.

Once inside, his hands are everywhere. The man is like an octopus.

"A drink. I think we need a drink," I shriek playfully at him.

"Sure, babe, what's your poison?" Lamond asks as he trails kisses down my neck.

"Bubbles. How about you get us both a glass?"

Lamond lightly kisses my lips, then disappears further into the house. I'm in a lounge room that is large enough to fit my whole home into. When he returns, he's carrying two glasses.

"Cristal... only the best for you."

I smile at Lamond and take the glass from him. He leans in and kisses me again, and I playfully push him away.

"I don't suppose you have any strawberries to go with this?" I ask, holding up my glass.

"As a matter of fact, I do." Lamond winks at me, places his glass on the coffee table, and goes back where he came from.

As soon as the door closes, I open my purse and tip the vial Angus gave me into his drink and quickly place it back into my clutch.

"I hope you can hear me, boys. The operation is a go," I whisper into my hidden mic.

The door swings open, and Lamond is there with my strawberries in a crystal bowl.

I saunter toward him, picking up his glass as I do and smile seductively. "Here's to a perfect evening."

He takes the glass, and I put mine to my lips swallowing its contents in one gulp. Lamond leers and copies me.

I take his glass off him and seductively walk him to the couch. He sits, and I take the bowl out of his hands, placing it on the coffee table. Lamond grabs me, pulls me to him, and then passes out cold.

"Thank God, the stuff worked as quick as you said it would. I'm on my way to the front door."

I walk back through his home and find Angus and Sean waiting for me as I open the door.

"Did you have to kiss him?" asks Sean angrily.

"He *thought* he was going to get lucky. You think I wanted his hands on me, let alone his mouth?" I shoot back.

Sean glares at me and pushes his way into the house. Angus shrugs at his brother and follows him.

"How long will he be out for?" I ask.

"An hour maybe a little longer," replies Angus.

The two of them go from room to room, putting bugs in all the phones and go through his home computer.

Angus is sitting in front of Lamond's laptop when he gets excited.

"What's up?" I ask, moving in to look over his shoulder.

"I need a pen."

Opening my evening bag, I give Angus a pen. He rips off a sheet of notepaper from the pad on the desk and writes something down.

"What is it?" I ask impatiently.

"It's a list of his contacts overseas who he's selling parts to."

"Why don't you copy the data?"

"I have, but this name here is in DC. I want to do a drive-by on the way home." Angus is smiling like a kid on Christmas morning.

"Okay, can we go now?" I ask impatiently.

Spark

"I'm with Cherie, can we roll?" chimes in Sean.

"Yeah, we've planted all the bugs, and I have a treasure trove to sift through," answers Angus as he holds up a flash drive.

Both Sean and I grin at him, and we head out of the house.

"Will he remember anything?" I ask.

"Nah, he'll have no memory after the drink. It's why Sean stripped him and put him to bed." Angus winks at me. "He'll think you were amazing."

I giggle as we walk down the sidewalk toward Angus' car. Sean's bike is parked behind it.

"You know you could ride with me?" Sean makes it a question, and I know if I get on, it'll mean so much more than a ride home.

"Not in this dress, I can't…" I pause and look him in the eye, "… and I don't think Maddock would like it very much."

Sean nods, quirks an eyebrow at me, and climbs on. "If you ever change your mind, you know where to find me."

I smile at him and get into the car.

CHAPTER 24

Maddock

It's been a week since Cherie and my brothers pulled their stunt and bugged Lamond's house. The pain in my shoulders and legs has decreased, and I can slowly move around. Cherie has been by my side the entire time, proving what a good woman she is.

Today she's sitting with the club whores, laughing as one of them tells her something in a hushed voice. I can't hear what's being said, but Cherie's face is one of amusement and shock. She catches me watching her, smiles at the ladies, and makes her way toward me.

"Hey, handsome, how are you feeling?"

"Better. What was so funny?"

Cherie's face goes bright red. "Maybe another time. What did you want to do today?"

Spark

I raise my eyebrows at her seductively, and her blush deepens. The only time we've been intimate was at my cabin back in Breckenridge, and try as I might, apart from kissing, she's been unwilling to go any further for fear of hurting me.

I give her my best lazy smile. "Hmmm, I could think of a few things… but how about we ring your granddaddy?"

Cherie smiles back at me, kisses me on the lips, and whispers, "That sounds good."

"Tease."

"You have no idea. Come on, which phone can I use?"

I hand her the prepaid cellphone Angus gave me and move away to let her have some privacy.

Kyle catches my eye, and I hobble toward him out the front of the clubhouse. "Good to see you up and moving, brother."

"Getting stronger every day. How's Angus doing with the surveillance?"

"I don't understand half of what he says, but the gist of it is, he's compiled enough evidence to put Lamond away for a long time."

"Good." I look down at my feet. Conversations with my brothers have been stilted. Not on their part, but mine. The guilt within me is all-consuming.

"We don't blame you, you know." I look into his eyes. "Heather is on Lamond. You did what you thought was right. It's all Da would have wanted. Heather wouldn't want you blaming yourself. She'd want you back with us. I've missed you, Mad."

"I've missed you all, too. It's been hell not being able to see all of you and knowing you all thought I was dead."

"Angus never believed it. He's waged his own personal war with the feds, trying to find you. You know he has mad skills, yeah?"

I grin. "Yeah, they recently showed me some photos of you all. In fact, one of them had you hooked up with a Lola?"

"Did they now?" Kyle shakes his head. "She's a hell of a woman, a real ball-breaker. The only woman who comes in here who won't let me get away with my bullshit. You'll like her, Lola's a straight shooter."

"So where is she?" I ask.

"Her mother is sick. She went home to take care of her. It's a long story, Mad, but *that* woman is lucky to have Lola, only she doesn't know it."

"Family can be complicated," I state.

"Doesn't have to be. Like I said, no one blames you." Kyle lightly punches me in the arm, which causes me to grimace. "Pussy."

"How about I stab you, then punch you in the arm and see how you like it?"

"Pussy." Kyle chuckles. "What are you going to do when this is all over?"

"I don't know. I haven't allowed myself to think too far into the future."

"Well, brother, now you have a future."

He's right, I do. I seek out Cherie, knowing she is part of it. Her face is a mask of seriousness. She's nodding her head vigorously while talking on the phone. When her eyes meet mine, I know something is wrong. I walk toward her, placing an arm around her. "What's wrong?"

"Granddaddy is being discharged, but he can't take care of the farm on his own. I need to go home." Her beautiful face is sad and anxious at the same time.

"I'll go with you."

"No, you won't," states Kyle from behind me.

I turn and scowl at him. "I wasn't asking for permission."

"Tough. Lamond knows where you were living. *You* can't go back."

Cherie places a hand on my arm. "Kyle's right, and do you really want to have to sit on a plane or a bus for hours? I'll be fine."

At the same time, Kyle and I say, "Bus?"

"I'm not sure I have enough money to fly back, so yes, bus," responds Cherie.

Kyle laughs and slaps my back. "Fuck! She doesn't know about you, does she? This one's a keeper."

Kyle walks away shaking his head and laughing. I glance at Cherie, and all she looks is confused.

"What don't I know now?"

"I have money, lots of it. I'll fly you back home."

"Like fuck you will," states Cherie.

"Babe, it's not a big deal."

"Ahh, yes, it is! I'm no one's whore."

Her language takes me by surprise.

I hold up both hands and take a step back. "Cherie, *you* are no one's whore. We got you here, and I'm going to get you home. I *will* tell *you* what you are." I reach up and touch her face. "You're beautiful, headstrong, and *mine*."

Cherie's face goes all soft, and she puts her arms around my waist, resting her head on my chest. "Okay," she whispers.

"Okay?" I ask.

Cherie leans back and looks up at me. "Yeah, okay."

"You're letting me off easy. Why?"

"Because you're right. Your family did get me here, I'm headstrong, and I am *yours*." Now, it's my turn to feel a rush of emotion. I tilt her head up and kiss her lips softly. Cherie breaks away. "But *you* are staying here."

I shake my head slightly.

"Your woman is right," chides Sean.

When I turn to look at him, he's staring at Cherie. "How so?"

"You're in no fit state to travel, and it's too dangerous. One of the MC could go with her, or I could go." Sean's eyes come back to me.

"Not you," I reply.

Sean grins and nods. "What about a prospect?"

"That I can live with."

"Hello! I'm in the room. You know I can take care of myself, right? Like who *didn't* get kidnapped? Hmmm? Oh, that would be *me*." With one had on her hip and the other one pointing at herself, she's as cute as hell.

I hold up my hands and take another step back which causes Sean to laugh. I shoot him a disapproving look then glance back at Cherie.

"Good point. But I *am* paying for your flight back. No arguments."

Cherie smiles and nods. "Deal."

CHAPTER 25

Maddock

"Mad, come on, it's time to go," orders Loch.

"Her plane hasn't left yet."

Loch sighs. "Dude, she can't see you. Come on. Besides, I want to buy you breakfast, and you can tell me about Boringridge."

"Breckenridge."

"Whatever."

I know he's right, and I'm behaving like a lovesick teenager. I nod, take one last look at her plane, and walk to the exit.

Loch is driving, and I take no notice of where we are headed until he stops the car. We're parked out front of our grandfather's favorite diner.

"I haven't been here in years."

Spark

Loch smiles and gets out, then leans on the roof of the car. "Neither have I. The others are waiting inside at Da's booth."

I don't wait for Loch to catch up as I stroll inside. Sitting in a booth in the back of the
restaurant are my brothers, and they all have a plate of food in front of them.

"You lot couldn't wait for us to get here?" I ask.

"We did wait. What took you so fucking long?" asks Kyle as he pours more maple syrup over his pancakes.

"Loverboy here had to wait till her plane left before he could leave," teases Loch.

I shake my head at them and sit down next to Jamie. "What's good here?"

"Everything," they all reply in unison.

The waitress comes over. She must be in her nineties, still spritely and all business.

"What can I get you, young man?"

"Pancakes with a side of bacon," I reply.

She looks at Loch over her glasses. "And you?"

"The same, please."

"Coffee?"

"Yes," I reply, and Loch nods.

She turns to go, stops, and turns back around. "Sure is nice to have the MacKenny men back in here." She points to a photograph on the wall. "I miss Kyle." Then she looks back at us and winks. "*He* was a good tipper."

I look around the table, and we are all grinning at her. Loch walks over to the picture, pulls it off the wall, and brings it back to us. It's a photograph of Da sitting in this booth smiling at the camera.

When the waitress comes back with coffee, I ask, "How come you have our Da up on the wall?"

"That man came in here every Sunday for breakfast and then again for lunch after church. When my Harry died, he'd call on me from time to time to make sure I was okay. Your granddaddy was good people. I miss him." She pats Kyle's shoulder. "And don't be late on Sunday."

I wait until she walks away, then ask, "What was that about?"

Kyle squirms in his seat and looks embarrassed. "Da had a soft spot for Annie. Near the end, he made me promise I'd look out for her, so, every week one of the boys or I take her to church. We pick her up from home, ask if she needs anything fixed while we're there, go to church with her, then bring her here. It's on a roster system. She was important to him, so she's important to the club."

"Damn, Kyle, why didn't you ever say anything?" asks Jamie.

Kyle shrugs. "I don't know. It felt like it was personal. Da didn't want anyone to know he'd been seeing Annie for a while. I think he felt like he was betraying Gran or rather we'd think that." Kyle shrugs again. "Da was sweet on her."

Spark

Annie comes back with our food. Loch gets up and takes it off her. "Annie, please sit down with us."

"I have work to do, son."

"Only for a minute," I interject.

Annie smiles at us, her blue eyes sparkling. "My break isn't for another hour. I'm no slacker. You boys will be back, so we can chat another time."

"How long has she worked here?" asks Loch as she walks away.

"Annie owns the place. She's only missed two days' work in her life," says a woman near the door. It's obvious she's related, same sparkling blue eyes. She walks over and holds out her hand to Loch.

"I'm Annette, Annie's my grandmother."

Loch rises and takes her hand. "Lochlan MacKenny, and this unruly bunch are my brothers."

Annette laughs. "I know who you are. Your Da showed me pictures, never seen you all together, though." She looks at Kyle. "Don't be late on Sunday."

Loch leans into her. "Actually, I'm taking her on Sunday."

"Well, don't be late. Enjoy your breakfasts." Annette smiles at us and moves away.

"*You* are going to take Annie to church? When was the last time you were *in* a church?" asks Jamie.

"You'll probably burst into flames as soon as you cross the threshold," teases Angus.

"Don't fuck with Annette," orders Kyle.

"Trust me when I tell you, brother, Annette isn't a woman you fuck with," says Sean.

Loch raises an eyebrow. "So you've tried, and she shut you down?"

"Fuck you."

"I'll take that as a yes."

"Enough! Eat your food. And Loch, leave Annette alone. You don't need another notch on your bedpost. If Da were alive, he'd tan your hide for even thinking about her that way. She *is* Annie's granddaughter," says Kyle.

"Jesus! Leave Loch alone. All he's doing is taking Annie to church. Don't overreact," I say defensively.

Sean begins to laugh, and Kyle is grinning and shaking his head.

"What?" I demand.

"You haven't changed. Still sticking up for your little brother who, by the way, can look after himself," jokes Angus.

I pick up my knife and fork and cut into my breakfast. "Whatever."

This causes all of them, including Loch, to laugh at me.

It's good to be with family.

CHAPTER 26

Maddock

It's early, and light is starting to trickle in from behind the curtains. My body is sore but healing. Cherie has been gone for three days. I spoke to her yesterday morning, and her grandfather is out of the hospital but not well. I've decided I'm going to hire someone to help look after his farm *if* Cherie and Mr. Lake will let me.

Slowly, I roll onto my side and sit up. I test the muscles in my arms and legs to see how they are feeling. Not as sore as yesterday, and the doctor is happy with the rate I'm progressing, but if you ask me, it's all taking too long.

Angus has enough information on Lamond to bury him, and he managed to record a conversation between him and an FBI agent. Special Agent Stephen Jamieson is as dirty as they come, which is good for us. If we don't turn him over, Kyle can use him to find out what they have on the club and hopefully get him to work for them.

I'm stretching my arms above my head when the door to my room bursts open.

"We've got a problem," states Angus, fear etched all over his face.

"Who?" I ask.

"Cherie."

My whole world spins out of control. I stand up and feel like I'm about to throw up or worse.

I frown at him. "She's back home, she's safe," I state.

"No. Lamond called last night. He has her."

"Last fucking night? And you didn't wake me? How?" I demand to know.

"We didn't know."

"But you're sure she's been taken?"

"Yeah, as I said, Lamond called. He put her on the phone." Angus looks stricken with fear and anger.

"What are the demands?" I ask quietly as my anger begins to rage inside of me.

"You, and the evidence you have on Lamond."

I look down at the floor, concentrating on slowly breathing in and out. I can't let Lamond win, but I can't let him hurt another person I love.

"Okay, let's do this."

"Mad, you can't give him what he wants."

"What choice do we have?"

Spark

"Sean has a plan."

"How long has Lamond had Cherie?" I demand to know as I imagine the horrors he's putting her through.

"Seven hours." I charge toward Angus, grabbing his shirt and pushing him against the wall out in the hallway. "We didn't tell you because *we knew* this is what you'd do. The only way to keep you safe and get Cherie back to us is your fucking family. *Don't shut us out again.*"

I let go of his shirt, and he slides back down the wall. Looking to my left, I see Kyle, Sean, Lochlan, and Jamie staring at me.

"We have a plan, brother, and it's a good one. Trust us," states Kyle.

I place my hand at the back of Angus' neck, staring into his eyes. I nod, and all the tension in his body drains away.

"The FBI agent is our way in. Trust me," states Angus.

"I do, brother, I do, but she's important."

"We know."

I feel helpless. My instinct is to go to Lamond and bargain for Cherie, but I know they are right. They'll kill both of us.

"I've called the agent who's on Lamond's payroll. He's setting up a meet with you, Lamond, and Cherie. We've picked the place, it's all worked out.

You just need to show up…" he points to our family and continues, "… we'll do the rest."

I nod. This all sounds too easy, like too many things could go wrong.

"When's it planned for?"

"Tonight. To make Lamond feel safe, we picked his place up near Bowie. It's private. And we have Rio to thank for a map of the place. Who knew such a big, burly guy would sell his grandmother to get out of the pit? This should be easy," replies Angus.

Easy.

Nothing ever is.

CHAPTER 27

Cherie

The drive up to my granddaddy's home is always something I look forward to. It's picturesque with the red barn and the white homestead. As the cab pulls up, my granddaddy comes out the front door. I jump out and engulf him in a hug.

"I've missed you," I gush.

"And I've missed you." He pushes me away and looks me in the eye. "How the hell did you meet Colton Anders?"

I burst out laughing. "It's a long story. Let me pay the cabbie, and we can sit down and chat."

Granddaddy nods and goes back inside the house while I pay and grab my bag. I stand on the porch and take in a deep breath. As much as I say I don't like it here, it's good to be home and on the land. The barn door is open and bangs noisily against the side of the building, and I frown. It's typically shut.

"Cherie… coffee's on," yells my granddaddy which causes me to smile, and I go inside.

As I walk into the kitchen, I notice he's lost weight and looks older to me. The way he's moving is a little slower, and he's breathing harder than normal.

I place a hand on his upper arm. "Are you okay?" I whisper.

"Yes, stupid doctors. Bloodsuckers! Money-hungry varmints."

"Sit down and tell me."

"The insurance didn't cover everything." Granddaddy puts down the spoon in his hand and stares out the kitchen window. "I think I'll have to sell the farm."

My breath catches in my throat as I watch him try and keep his composure. This land has been in my family for generations. My grandfather has never lived anywhere else. This is home.

"How about I bake some cookies, and we can sit down and talk? You always said a problem shared is a problem halved."

He nods and sits at the kitchen table. "Chocolate chip?"

"If you have 'em."

Granddaddy nods and points to the fridge. "I was hoping you'd make me some."

"So that's the reason you wanted me home," I tease.

"It's one of them. Now, Colton Anders?"

I laugh as I get out the ingredients for the cookies. "He's a friend of Maddock's brother, Lochlan. Oh my God, Granddaddy, he was divine. Such a nice guy."

"Maddock's brother, Lochlan? Who the hell are they?"

I stop and look at him. "There's a lot to tell you. Eric, the mechanic, is Maddock. Lochlan, well... he's his brother."

Even to my ears, this sounds ridiculous.

"Eric is Maddock?" I nod. "And he's the reason you went to DC?"

"Yes. It's kind of confusing. See Eric Hill is really Maddock MacKenny. He was, I mean is... well, sort of... in witness protection."

Granddaddy frowns, shakes his head, and rubs the back of his neck. "I need coffee."

I smile and nod. "Okay, coming right up."

I pour him a cup and continue with my cookie preparations.

"You like him?" he asks.

"Colt Anders?"

"No, I mean, Eric or Maddock, but do you like Colton? There was a picture of him kissing you."

I laugh. "No. I like Maddock. I think I've finally picked a winner."

"He does seem like a good one," he replies. "Why was he in witness protection?"

"The man he was working for was selling parts to an arms dealer. Maddock found out, and they tried to kill him but ended up killing his sister instead."

"Lord have mercy. They killed his sister?"

"Yeah, so sad." I shake my head.

"It explains why he has no friends. How'd they find him?"

I pause and look down at the dough between my fingers. "While he was visiting you, Maddock ran into a man who recognized his tattoo." I glance over at my granddaddy, and he's looking into his coffee cup. "It wasn't your fault."

His eyes meet mine. "I know that." Granddaddy takes a sip of coffee. "He seems like a good man. So, tell me about Colt Anders."

I giggle. "It was all a ploy to make sure Maddock is safe and a rather long story. Colt is a super nice guy," I say, smiling goofily.

"You sure your not interested in Colt?"

"I'm sure. He's larger than life and a player. Maddock is hardworking and a good guy." I bend and place the cookies in the oven. I'm about to sit down when I hear the barn door bang. "Dang it! The barn door is open."

"Must've come loose, I'll go shut it."

"No, you won't. You sit there and watch my cookies, and in twelve minutes the buzzer's going off. If I'm not back, pull them out."

"Yes, ma'am," replies Granddaddy with a grin.

I shake my head and head toward the barn.

As I walk in the direction of the banging red door, nothing seems out of place. My mind is on my granddaddy and how I'm going to help him. I grab the door with both hands and push. Suddenly, a hand goes over my mouth. My reaction is to kick back as hard as I can. A yelp escapes my assailant, and he releases me. I run inside the barn and into the arms of someone else. He's taller than me, and his arms feel like a vice around me.

"Calm the fuck down, or we'll kill the old man."

I stop fighting instantly, and he lets me go. I take a step back, ball my hand into a fist, and hit him as hard as I can. The man's head turns with my punch. He rubs his jaw and looks back at me, anger in his eyes. He raises his fist and strikes me in the jaw. I feel myself falling, pain explodes, and my head whacks the floor of the barn, hard. The last thing I see before my world goes black is a boot to the face.

CHAPTER 28

Sean

The shack I'm working out of has no air conditioning, and sweat drips from my forehead. It's fiddly work, and my hand shakes. I stop, take a deep breath, slow my breathing, and insert the last wire with a steady hand. Now is not the time to lose my nerve.

All the while as I work, Heather and Cherie plague my thoughts. I live by a code. It's a simple one—you don't fuck with my family or those I care about. I know the others won't understand why I'm doing this, but I *have* to.

When it's done, I carefully attach it to the large magnet. Normally, this work is done without gloves, but I'm not risking getting caught. It's taken longer to assemble, but I'm happy with the result. I place the package into my backpack, clean up my worktable, and open the door to see Kyle headed in my direction. I place the backpack on my shoulder and walk toward him.

"Hey, man," I offer as a greeting, trying to sound casual.

"You ready for tonight? It should all go off like clockwork," replies Kyle.

I grin. "Yeah, man, I'm ready." Kyle slaps my arm, and the backpack jostles. I grimace, and he eyes me curiously. "I'm worried about Cherie."

Kyle places his hands on his hips. "She's not yours to worry about," he says flatly.

"Not like that, man. I know she belongs to Mad. I don't want to lose anyone else to that fuckwad, Lamond."

Kyle's hands fall from his hips, and he nods. "Yeah, I get you."

I walk toward my bike with Kyle shadowing me. "Where you going?"

"I thought I might head up early, take the long way, so I don't run into anyone and scope out the place."

"Good idea, you want me to go with?"

"No, man. I'll be cool. It's easier for me to get in and out alone without anyone tagging along." The lies fall from my lips, and my brother, my President, believes me.

Kyle nods. "Okay, check back in after you get there and again within an hour. If I don't hear from you, we're all coming."

I nod, put my backpack on properly, and start my bike.

I watched Lamond pull up, alone, and walk into his house. Two men arrive shortly after and with a limp body that I assume is Cherie. It was still daylight when I crept under the car. I wanted to help Cherie, but I was scared I'd get her killed. The plan to get her out should work. What I'm doing right now, that's another story.

The wires are all attached, and the magnet is glued to the gas tank. The explosion should happen five seconds after the ignition turns on.

I wait in the dirt listening for footsteps or voices, long after they've gone inside. There is nothing. Sliding out from under the car, I carefully go back into the woods. No one has seen me. All my training in the Marines prepared me for this. Darkness slowly falls, the men have since left, and another man arrives. From the distance I'm at, it looks like the fed Angus showed me a picture of. There are no screams from Cherie or loud voices inside. I hope she's still alive. When I'm sure I can't be seen, I jog the mile to the rendezvous spot. Some of the MC are here already.

"How was it?" asks Kyle.

"From what I could see, it's Lamond, the fed, and Cherie inside."

Kyle nods and places his phone to his ear. "You ready?" He looks down at the ground and nods again. "We have men placed everywhere. Sean just got back, and he's confident it's Lamond, the fed, and Cherie in the house. Good luck, brother."

I go and sit by myself, arms crossed over my chest as we wait. Kyle thinks I'm worried about Cherie and leaves me to my exile.

There's nothing left for me to do but wait.

CHAPTER 29

Maddock

It's nearly midnight as I pull up in front of Lamond's home. It's off the beaten path, no neighbors, and before I get out of the car, I scan my surroundings. I know there are MC all over the place, but I have no idea if Lamond has men waiting for me too. I let out a deep breath and open the door. Slowly, I stand, pausing to see if anyone rushes out. When no one does, I reach back in and grab a briefcase with all of the evidence against Lamond inside.

Every noise is amplified as I make my way to the front door. I'm dressed in a dark blue suit, white shirt, and brown shoes. This is what I used to wear every day to work. It all feels alien to me now. I guess after three years of wearing grease, jeans, boots, and T-shirts, I'm out of practice.

Spark

The front door opens, and I stop in my tracks. A man in his thirties steps out. He's got sandy blond hair and is wearing a black suit and white shirt. His expression is grim like he doesn't want to be here. Our eyes meet, and he does a chin lift. I continue my approach.

"You must be the elusive Maddock MacKenny?"

"Yeah, and you are?"

"It's not important." He pauses, looking behind me into the darkness. I turn around, unable to see anything or anyone. I look back at him and raise an eyebrow. He shrugs, moves back inside the house, opening the door wider. "Please come in."

This house is not a little holiday home. I'm in the foyer, and if Rio's plan of the house is correct, the oversized office should be to the right of the front door. The man closes the front door and gestures for me to go left, which should take me into the first of three living rooms.

As I enter, my eyes go to Cherie who's sitting in a chair, shoulders rigid, back straight, and her face is bruised. I take a step toward her, and she practically leaps out of the chair and into my arms. Cherie is shaking uncontrollably. I drop the briefcase and hold on tight.

"Isn't that sweet?" says Lamond snidely from further into the room.

I look down at Cherie. "Did he hurt you?"

Lamond replies, "That little cunt wouldn't stop screaming, so they had to subdue her. Apart from the bruises you see, she hasn't been harmed."

I ignore him and look into Cherie's eyes. "Did he hurt you?"

Cherie shakes her head, and I let out the breath I didn't realize I'd been holding. I nod at her and position her behind me. Cherie understands. I feel her head between my shoulder blades, and her hands on my waist. She's scared, but she's okay.

The man who let me in gets the briefcase and hands it to Lamond. Lamond smirks, opens it, and goes through the files inside.

"Is this all of it?" he asks.

"Yeah, that's all of it."

"You know Special Agent Stephen Jamieson here..." he points to him, "... destroyed all the evidence they had on me, but I knew you would have covered your ass. Why couldn't you leave things alone and then none of this... unpleasantness would have happened, and your sister, Heather, would still be alive."

"Don't *you* say her name," I hiss.

Lamond laughs, the FBI agent flinches.

"And as for your little friend there, if she hadn't left her pen behind, I'd never have known something was wrong. What did you hope to accomplish by getting her to break into my home?"

"I wanted my life back."

Spark

"You must know everything on my computer is password protected. What did you think you'd get out of it?"

"You know one of my brothers is a hacker, right?"

Lamond still looks confident, but Special Agent Jamieson looks angry as he peers down at Lamond.

"You can go," states Lamond.

"That's it? I can go?"

"Yes, I have everything I want. After I burn all of this..." Lamond stands and points to the briefcase, "... there's not a lot the U.S. government can do to me. Your word isn't enough to convict me on if there's no proof."

I can feel Cherie move away from me, pulling at my coat, coaxing me to step backward.

"How do I know you'll leave me, us, alone?"

"You don't," states Lamond. "But I have no interest in hurting you. I never did. It's business, that's all. Nothing personal."

He killed my sister, and it's nothing personal?

He kidnapped my woman, and it's nothing personal?

If Cherie weren't with me, I'd rip the fucker apart.

Keeping my mouth shut, I back out of the living room into the foyer. Once there, I turn, open the front door, tuck Cherie into my side and walk her quickly to the car.

Opening the driver's door, Cherie jumps in and crawls across the seat to the passenger side with me sliding into the driver's seat in one fluid movement. I grip her face with my hands and crush her mouth to mine.

"Are you okay?" I whisper.

"Yes. Some of his goons got me going out to the barn. Does Granddaddy know I'm safe?"

I'm nodding at her, turning on the car and backing out of the driveway without breaking eye contact.

"Buckle up," I order. "Your granddaddy is fine. I called Theo and asked him to check on him. He was concerned, but you know he's a tough old bugger. He'll be okay."

Cherie does as she's told, nodding and smiling. A tear trickles down her face, but now is not the time to comfort her. I'm driving like a madman to get to the rendezvous spot with my brothers and the MC. It's only a mile away, but until I'm with them, I won't feel protected.

When we pull up, Sean rips open Cherie's door and helps her out. His eyes go deadly as he takes in her bruised face. "Motherfucker!" Sean hisses.

"I'm okay."

Sean looks into her eyes searching for something. I put my arm around Cherie, and she buries her face once again in my chest. Sean nods and walks away. There's a look in his eyes which bothers me. It's the same look he came home with after his first deployment. Deadly.

"It all went smoothly. Your FBI man was there."

"Yeah, he's our FBI agent now. You should see the shit Angus has on the fucker," replies Kyle with a grin.

"How do we know Lamond won't come after me or us again?"

"Mad, we have enough on him to give to the feds. He's going to prison for a long time," says Angus.

"It's not enough," states Sean.

"Brother, we've talked about this. For Mad to be free and clear, Lamond has to face charges. We'll get him in prison," says Kyle with authority in his voice.

"He gets to breathe free and clear until then? Nah, brother, it doesn't work for me."

"Sean—"

An explosion lights up the night sky. All of us turn toward the fireball that quickly disappears.

Cherie looks at Sean. "What have you done?"

"What I needed to do."

En masse, we all head for Lamond's house.

Sitting on the lawn is Special Agent Stephen Jamieson. He looks shell-shocked.

Kyle is the first to get to him. "What the fuck happened?"

Jamieson is staring at what used to be a car. Parts of it are scattered all over the place, some embedded in the front of the house.

"What the fuck happened?" yells Jamieson. "You fucking bastards is what the fuck happened. You had him. With my cooperation, he was going away for a fucking long time. How do I explain this?" he asks as he gets to his feet pointing at the wreckage.

Everyone has dismounted from their bikes or cars and have surrounded Jamieson. Kyle whistles and points in the air and does a circle with his hand, and all MC members get back on their bikes and ride out.

Sean walks up to Jamieson and pokes his chest. "You're going to find components in the debris which will point to Lamond's other business partners." Sean pushes a file onto Jamieson. "In this file that you were coming out here to talk to Lamond about, you have enough evidence to bury him and get my brother, Maddock, home from the middle of fucking nowhere. And Special Agent Stephen Jamieson, remember... *you* work for *us*."

Kyle is furious. Sean avoids looking at any of us as he mounts his bike. None of us knew he was capable of this. It's only the MacKenny clan, Cherie, and Jamieson left standing outside.

Sean looks down at his bike, then looks up at all of us. "It was for Heather. I couldn't... I wouldn't let the fucker take another breath." He starts his bike and rides away.

We all stand there watching him ride down the lane, the only noise is the crackling of the fire.

"Fuck," mutters Kyle. "We need to book. Jamieson, you onboard?"

"Do I have a choice?"

"No, you fucking don't," replies Kyle in a deadly tone. "Let's go! We need to be gone."

Shell-shocked, I get into the car as does Cherie. We drive in silence for a while.

Cherie reaches across and links her fingers with mine. "Maddock, where are we going?"

"Home."

"And where's home?"

"For now, Breckenridge. We need to see your grandfather and get some things settled. I need to heal, and we have to figure out what our next step is."

"I had no idea Sean was going to do it."

"None of us did. Sean has his own brand of justice, and truthfully, I'm glad the fucker's dead. I know one thing. I can't go back to my old life, and I have no idea what I want to do now that I can do whatever I want. Does that make sense?"

"Yes, love, it does."

"I know one thing, whatever happens, I want you by my side. Are you down with that?"

Without hesitation, Cherie answers, "Yes."

CHAPTER 30

Angus

I waited a day before I leaked the story to the news. Making sure Maddock is safe from all persecution from the authorities was first and foremost in my mind. The press is so gullible. Most of them don't even bother to check the facts before they run the story. He's been portrayed as a hero going up against the bad guy who got taken out by the very people he was supplying. I'm grinning as I walk into the clubhouse.

Kyle lets out a whistle gaining my attention, and I walk toward him, holding up the newspaper.

"You see this?" Kyle nods. "We have a bonafide hero in our family." I laugh, and Kyle joins in.

"You did good, little brother."

"Yeah. Has Sean showed up yet?"

Kyle's face clouds over, and he shakes his head. I'm not sure what he's going to do to Sean, but I know he's not happy with him.

"It all worked out," I state.

"Yeah, it did. But what if Lamond had put Mad and Cherie into his car? What if—"

"It all worked *out*," I repeat more forcefully.

"He got *lucky*."

"Yeah, but it worked." I shrug and ask, "Does Mad know what I've done?"

"With the press? Nah, figured when he finally gets back to Breckenridge, they'd be waiting for him."

"Why haven't you told him?"

"I'm glad Mad is back, but he needs to figure out where he'll end up. Of course, I want him here, but he's a grown man. He'll find his way."

"It'd be nice if he stayed with us for a while. Seems like Jamie and Loch are going to stay for a bit."

"And you?"

"Yeah, I'm keeping close to home until this thing blows over. I don't need my face out in the media. All the attention makes it hard for me to do what I do."

"And what exactly is that, brother?"

I grin at Kyle. "A bit of this and a bit of that."

CHAPTER 31

Maddock

We take our time on the trip, perfectly happy in our bubble. No distractions, just Cherie and me. If I'm honest with myself, I'd keep driving and not face what's coming. I don't want to deal with the authorities or Mr. Lake or even my family who I was so desperate to get back to.

It's taken over a week to get here. I'm about to pull into the driveway of Mr. Lake's property—time to face the music. As we pass the barn, I see a whole bunch of cars and vans parked in front of the main house.

When we pull up, they all come running, and I realize it's the press.

I lock eyes with Cherie. "Shit, babe, I'm sorry."

Spark

At the last gas station, Cherie purchased a newspaper with my face and the story splashed on the front page.

She shakes her head and smiles. "It's cool. But you need to get them off our land. I'm surprised Granddaddy hasn't shot any of them."

As if he can sense his granddaughter's arrival, Mr. Lake appears on the porch, looking disgruntled.

"I'll see what I can do."

Cherie hooks a hand around my neck and pulls me in. She kisses me chastely, pulls back, and runs her hand up and down my neck. "Be nice."

"Babe, I'm always nice."

Cherie's smile broadens, and she laughs. "Yeah, right."

With a sigh, she opens the car door and steps out. The press flock around her, taking photographs, yelling out questions. I wait until she reaches Mr. Lake. Even from here, the love he has for her shines out.

"Mr. MacKenny! How does it feel to be alive and have everyone know?"

A ripple of laughter goes through the crowd. I smile and make my way up to the porch.

"You two go inside," I say quietly to Cherie and Mr. Lake. Turning around, I face the hungry pack of people, screaming out questions.

I raise my hands, motioning them to quiet down. "Hello... if you could all calm down?" I pause and look out at them. When they become quiet, I continue, "Yes, I'll answer your questions but not here." As a whole, their voices rise. "Enough," I yell.

I look out over the crowd and see a police cruiser making its way toward us. It pulls up, and the local sheriff gets out, and so does U.S. Marshal Maria Lovett.

All eyes go to the sheriff, and Maria makes a beeline toward me.

"Folks, last time I checked, you all are on private land, and I'm pretty sure the owner didn't invite you. So, please, pack up all your gear and clear out. Mr. MacKenny here is scheduled to give you all an interview in the town hall tomorrow at noon. Now, get," orders the sheriff.

"How about we go inside, Maddock, and let the sheriff handle this while you answer a few questions?" I look into Maria's eyes and see anger.

Great. Just what I need, a U.S. Marshal pissed at me. I grin at her, open the front door, and motion for her to go inside. I stalk past her and head toward the voices further into the house.

I find Cherie in the kitchen, apron on, laughing with her grandfather. The smile falls off her face when she sees Maria behind me. I place my arm around Cherie and pull her into my side.

"Cherie, Mr. Lake... meet U.S. Marshal Maria Lovett. My handler."

Spark

Cherie breaks away from me, holding out her hand. "Welcome to Breckenridge and my granddaddy's home."

Maria gives Cherie a courtesy nod, shakes her hand, and fixes me with a death stare.

"Where the hell have you been?" demands Maria.

Cherie backs away and into my arms. Instinctively, I wrap them around her.

"U.S. Marshal Lovett, how are you?"

"MacKenny, I swear if you had—"

"Calm down. Cherie and I went on a road trip, that's all. How the fuck did the reporters know who I am?" I ask, feigning innocence and going on the defense.

"Wait, you had nothing to do with Lamond's death?"

"Lamond is dead?"

"Come on, Maddock! Your little girlfriend there was seen in a club that Lamond frequents. Are you trying to tell me you know *nothing* about this?"

I turn to face Cherie. "You went to Washington?"

"Yes, honey, I told you about the modeling gig and Colton Anders. You remember?"

With my back to Maria, I wink at Cherie.

"The Colton Anders' thing?" I turn around and stare at Maria. "Yeah, she told me about that. What does that have to do with Lamond?"

"You seriously don't know?" asks Maria skeptically.

I let out a frustrated sigh, scrub my hand over my face, and glare back at Maria who quirks an eyebrow at me in disbelief, then shakes her head slowly.

"Lamond is dead. It looks like a terrorist bombing, and we found enough evidence at his home to go after the people he was selling parts to." Maria pauses. "You really don't know *anything*?"

"Would I be here in the middle of fucking nowhere if I did?"

"Language," shouts Mr. Lake.

Suppressing a grin, I nod at Mr. Lake. "No, Maria, I have no idea what you're talking about."

Maria throws her hands up in the air and taps her foot.

There's a knock at the front door followed by, "Anyone home? Samuel?"

"In the kitchen, Sheriff," yells out Mr. Lake.

The sheriff takes off his hat as he comes into the room.

"Coffee?" asks Mr. Lake.

"That'd be good, Sam. Got those reporters to move on. Sorry it took me so long to get out here, but Ms. Lovett wanted to come talk to you."

Cherie pours the sheriff a cup and holds up an empty mug to me. I nod.

"That'd be Marshal Lovett, and yes, I wanted to ask you about Maddock, but here he is in the flesh."

Maria looks me up and down, discord and unhappiness etched into her features.

I smile at the sheriff and hold out my hand. "Maddock MacKenny formerly Eric Hill. I don't think we've ever had the pleasure," I say with a grin as we shake hands.

CHAPTER 32

Cherie

His muscles ripple every time he raises the ax over his head as he cuts the wood in two. It's colder here now, but Maddock has worked up a sweat and removed his T-shirt. I'm sitting on a window seat, a soft blue blanket wrapped around me with a coffee in hand as I watch him work outside. My shiny red Mustang glistens in the sun at the front of the house. I had no idea my grandfather was having it restored for me. He is the only one in my family who has ever given a damn about me.

The press hail Maddock as a hero, the one who stood up against big business, and although he lost everything, he has come out on top. There were so many questions from the press about Heather and me. The five MacKenny boys were pursued relentlessly until another big scandal erupted.

Spark

Occasionally, a reporter will approach us, and although Maddock is polite, he's no longer doing interviews or discussing it further.

Maddock takes one last swing, embedding the ax into the block and walks toward the house. We are at my granddaddy's home. It's funny, I never wanted to live with my granddaddy, but Maddock has made it work. The hospital bills were paid for, and even though we've never talked about it, I know Maddock paid for them. He's stopped working at the garage. Theo was pissed at first, then offered him twice his normal pay if he'd stay. Maddock politely declined, but he did offer his services as an accountant and financial adviser.

Today, we are leaving for London—the first stop on a very long tour of the world. Maddock is in no hurry to go back to his life, and he understands I have to make sure my granddaddy is safe and well. So, we've planned for him to travel with us until he has had enough. Then Maddock's brothers are going to check up on him while we are gone.

"Hey, beautiful, is there any more coffee?"

"Yes, just made a pot."

The T-shirt is back on, and I watch as he quickly pours himself a cup, drags a chair next to me, and pulls me in for a quick kiss.

"You been watching me?"

"Yeah, nice view," I purr.

Maddock smiles, eyes sparkling, cupping my face with one hand. "Wanna go back to bed?"

My body responds like it always does, nerve endings already on fire. "You could persuade me…"

Maddock stands, takes my cup from me, and places both mugs on the kitchen table. Then he bends, picks me up, and takes me into our bedroom.

His touch elicits a wonderous heat which spreads throughout my being. Our lovemaking has turned slow and deliberate. We enjoy taking our time and exploring each other, but this morning I have other ideas.

Maddock lays me on the bed and strips off, the sight of him naked fueling my desire. I'm only wearing socks and a big sweater, both of which come off quickly. His mouth finds mine as he lays down, covering my body with his own.

"You're all sweaty." I giggle.

"Promise to make you the same," Maddock teases back.

The kiss turns from soft and sweet to a passionately burning fire. Tongues entwined, I groan as his hand moves down my body, and when his fingers find my sweet spot, I twist my head, arch up, and beg for more.

"Don't stop!"

Maddock kisses down my throat, making his way to my nipple where he sucks and flicks it with his tongue.

Spark

"I need you, now."

Maddock chuckles. "I aim to please."

His fingers torment me for a moment longer, then I'm flipped over, pulled up on my knees as his cock impales me to the hilt in one fluid movement.

That first penetration is always the best and a shock to my system, and I always gasp.

Maddock stays still. I rock forward and back, enjoying the feel of his cock as it goes in and out of me. His hands stroke my back, then grip my hips, fingers digging in pleasantly as he moves me faster.

"Fuck, you feel good... made for me," groans Maddock.

I reach down and work myself, feeling electricity build between my legs. I know I'm close.

"Come for me, baby," orders Maddock.

And I do as I'm told. The orgasm washes over me as I buck against him wantonly. His fingers dig deeper into me, heightening my experience.

Maddock groans, thrusting into me one more time as he too reaches his orgasm.

Slowly, his fingers release their hold, and he strokes up and down the backs of my legs.

"I could do that to you for the rest of my life."

A warmth which starts in my chest and ends up with me getting all emotional. Tears fall, and I make a hiccupping sound.

Maddock pulls out and lays down beside me, pulling me onto his chest. "Why the tears?" Maddock asks.

"Happy tears," I whisper.

"You sure?"

I nod and push up on one elbow to look down at him. "Yes, lover. You're making a lot of my dreams come true."

"But not all?"

I twist and sit up with my back against the headboard. Maddock does the same.

"I have things I'd like to do, and although I appreciate everything you're doing, I'm going to need to pay you back."

"Need to pay me back?" I nod at him, and he frowns. "Cherie, you don't need to pay me back. I don't care if you never pay me back."

"No, you don't get it, I—"

Maddock holds a finger to my lips. "No, beautiful, it's *you* who doesn't get it. I have a lot of money. I have no idea what I'm going to do, but I've made some wise investments and might play the stock market for a while. And, babe, we're a team. Your goals are my goals. We're in this *together*."

My stomach does a flip, and more tears well in my eyes threatening to fall.

"To… together?" I blubber.

"Yeah, babe. For as long as you want me."

Spark

My tears fall. "Forever."
"Done."

EPILOGUE

Sean

I shadowed Maddock and Cherie back to Breckenridge. Slept rough and stayed out of sight, but I needed to make sure he was okay and out of danger. Now that the story has broken, he'll be safe. Angus is good at making people look in one direction when the truth can be under your nose.

It's been a month since I've seen Kyle. I know he's angry, so I need him to calm down before I go back. And I am going back. Well, I keep telling myself I am.

I'm sitting on Maddock's front porch waiting for him to come home. He's mostly been staying with Cherie at her grandfather's. No one has come to town, apart from the reporters who harassed him. I took photographs of all the people he came into contact with and sent them to Angus—everyone checked out.

I hear the sound of a Harley and look up. Mad is on his way up the hill. He's alone, and I'm glad. I need to talk to him without Cherie around.

I'm watching his face as he climbs off his bike. He looks grim. I stand as he mounts the steps two at a time. When he reaches me, he engulfs me in a hug, holding tight to the back of my neck.

"Thank God you're okay."

"Mad, I'm sorry."

Maddock releases me and steps back. "That's something you never have to say to me, brother. You did what you felt you needed to do, and I can't say I'm sorry he's dead." I nod. "The others are worried, you need to call in."

"Kyle will be disappointed."

"Yes, he will, but he'll get over it."

I nod and place my hands in my pockets. "Got a beer?"

Maddock grins. "I think so." He opens his front door. "Come in, take a load off."

I follow him inside and sit at his kitchen table. "What are you going to do now?"

Mad smiles. "They've finally released my money back to me. I'm going to take Cherie on a very long holiday with her grandfather. It should be… interesting."

I chuckle. "Whipped."

"In the best possible way. What about you?"

"Going to visit an old army buddy in Texas. I need to put some space between Kyle and me, for a while."

"You're family. He'll get over it."

"He might forgive me as his brother, but as his VP?" I shake my head. "Probably not."

"You're not going to know unless you talk to him."

"Did you have a beer or not?"

Maddock nods and opens his fridge, pulling out two cold ones. He hands me one and sits down next to me.

"To family."

We both twist off our tops.

"To family."

The ride to my old sergeant's house takes me the better part of a month. I feel like a coward, but I can't face Kyle. We've spoken on the phone, and he asked me to come back in, but I used my old sergeant as a bullshit excuse, said he needed some help on his farm. Truth is, he doesn't even know I'm coming.

Spark

Last I heard from Sergeant Thomas Trent was he was running cattle on his family's ranch. We were close when we were both in. I saved his life, and he saved mine on numerous occasions.

I pull into the local gas station, and an older guy comes out. "Fill 'er up?"

"Sure, man, you good to do it?" I ask.

"Yep."

I wait until he's finished, and we both walk back into the gas station.

"You know where I can find the Trent Ranch?"

"Tom's place?"

"Yeah, he's an old buddy of mine."

The old guy scoffs. "I doubt that. Tom's got no friends. Not anymore, leastways. That'll be twenty-three dollars and seventy cents."

I hand over three ten-dollar notes. "Keep the change. And where did you say the Trent Ranch is?"

"I didn't."

I put both hands on the counter and lean over. "Well, how about you tell me now."

The old guy looks me up and down. "The Trent Ranch is ten miles further down the road. Take the first road on the left, then the second right and keep going, you'll find it. But you won't find Tom there."

"Why's that?"
"Thomas Trent is dead."

TO BE CONTINUED

in

Book Two, *Spark of Vengeance*, the MacKenny Brothers Series

Spark

If you liked this story, you might also like:

The Savage Angels MC Series

Savage Stalker Book 1
BLURB

Isn't it funny?

How one accident can change your entire path.

I was an international rock star and the female lead singer for the Grinders, but now I'm hiding in the mountains away from everything and everyone.

That is until the President of the Savage Angels MC, Dane Reynolds gave me a reason to feel again.

He's fierce, strong and loyal, but someone sinister hides in the shadows.

Can Dane save Kat? Or will the savage stalker get to her first?

Savage Fire Book 2
Savage Town Book 3
Savage Lover Book 4

Kathleen Kelly

Savage Sacrifice Book 5
Savage Rebel (Novella) Book 6
Savage Lies Book 7
Savage Life Book 8
Savage Christmas (Novella) Book 9
Savage Angels MC Collection Books 1 – 3
Savage Angels MC Collection Books 4 – 6

The Grinders Series

Truth Book One

ACKNOWLEDGMENTS

For my readers who have the utmost faith in me, thank you.

To all my author friends, you know who you are. I am blessed to know you.

My street team, Kelly's Angels, you are an amazing bunch. Your continued support and friendship means the world to me.

Bloggers in the Indie book world – I love you. If you didn't share my books or review them, no one would know about them or buy them. THANK YOU.

And to you, the reader who purchased my latest book, thank you. It has taken over twelve months and much agonizing for this to come to print. I hope you are going to love the MacKenny Brothers as much as I do. Please contact me on FB or send me an email to let me know what you think, good or bad.

> "A reader lives a thousand lives before he dies.
> The man who never reads lives only one."
> – George RR Martin.

CONNECT WITH ME ONLINE

Check these links for more books from
Author Kathleen Kelly

READER GROUP

Want access to fun, prizes and sneak peeks?
Join my Facebook Reader Group.
https://bit.ly/32X17pv

NEWSLETTER

Want to see what's next?
Sign up for my Newsletter.
http://eepurl.com/-x035

GOODREADS

Add my books to your TBR list
on my Goodreads profile.
http://bit.ly/1xsOGxk

Spark

AMAZON
Buy my books from my Amazon profile.
https://amzn.to/2JCUT6q

WEBSITE
https://kathleenkellyauthor.com/

TWITTER
https://twitter.com/kkellyauthor

INSTAGRAM
https://instagram.com/kathleenkellyauthor

EMAIL
2linden2@tpg.com.au

FACEBOOK
https://bit.ly/36jlaQV

ABOUT THE AUTHOR

Kathleen Kelly was born in Penrith, NSW, Australia. When she was four, her family moved to Brisbane, QLD, Australia. Although born in NSW she considers herself a QUEENSLANDER!

She married her childhood sweetheart, and they live in Toowoomba with their fur baby.

Kathleen enjoys writing contemporary, romance novels with a little bit of erotica. She draws her inspiration from family, friends, and the people around her. She can often be found in cafes writing and observing the locals.

If you have any questions about her novels or would like to ask Kathleen a question, she can be contacted via e-mail:

kathleenkellyauthor@gmail.com

or she can be found on Facebook. She loves to be contacted by those who love her books.

Printed in Great Britain
by Amazon